My Crazy Girl

Reluctant Feminization with College Sweetheart

"This story is for you and Kim Ho-sik.

May it transform you into

the person you are meant to be and

transport you into a world

where your fantasies come to life."

BRIGHTLUCKY PRESS

This book is a work of fiction. Any resemblance to actual persons, living or dead, or actual events is purely coincidental. All the characters are within the legal age of consent. The author and publisher disclaim any liability, loss, or risk incurred as a consequence, directly or indirectly, of the use and application of any of the contents of this book.

This book is intended for mature audiences and contains adult themes and language. Reader discretion is advised.

If you have any questions regarding the use or distribution of this book, please contact the author directly. Thank you for respecting the author's work and intellectual property rights.

Table of Contents

∞∞∞

My Crazy Girl

Table of Contents

Introduction

Free Vip Mailing List

Chapter 1

Chapter 2

Chapter 3

Chapter 4

Chapter 5

Chapter 6

Chapter 7

Chapter 8

Chapter 9

Chapter 10

Chapter 11

Epilogue

Book Bundles

Custom Story

Audiobooks

Sissy Store

Other Titles

Author's Message

Introduction

"I really love her. But she's crazy, almost batshit, to the point where she asked me to wear her high-heeled pumps during one of our dates!"

This is an illustrated romance novella, it includes beautiful images inside. Enjoy!

People say navigating college life was like voluntarily signing up for four years of sleepless studying and drunken nights. They were right, and I was luckily able to handle it.

Up until one night when I met that drunk girl in the subway station, my crazy girl that showed me how twistedly beautiful this world could be and left me questioning if I was ready for it.

Clutch your Pearl Necklace Tight and

Prepare for a Transgender Romance Ride!

Note: This story contains transgender love, feminization, transgender romance, and first time with a transgender woman tropes. Some real places and people were referenced but the story is a work of fiction. The cover image is from Brightlucky Press.

I'm Lilly Lustwood and I'm a transgender woman. I'm a senior editor by day and I recall and write my romantic rendezvous by night.

Most of my titles deal with feminization. A fragment of what makes me find happiness in my gender identity, amidst the discrimination against women like me is my transformation.

When I look in the mirror and I gaze at my authentic self, I know that no matter what happens, I'm living my life and not somebody else's idea of how I should.

The clothes I wear, my long black hair, the fruity bath products that I use, the hormone medications I take before I go to bed, the sillage of my floral perfume, the surgeries I've undergone, and every step that I take with my size 12 Jimmy Choos, are all proudly from me...

...from my authentic feminine self.

Picture this...

- ❖ I have long and straight black hair and stand 5ft 6in.
- ❖ My alabaster curvaceous physique enjoys silk dresses
- ❖ I'm blessed with huge cat eyes and heart-shaped lips
- ❖ I want to share the rest but that's not very lady-like *wink*

Now that you know what your storyteller looks like, let's get to My Crazy Girl.

Free Vip Mailing List

∞∞∞

Before we get to the exciting part, I'm cordially inviting you to be a Lilly Lustwood VIP.

IT DOESN'T COST ANYTHING. All you have to do is Join my Mailing List.

I will be sending you FREE Exclusive Romantic Content that you won't find anywhere else.

My First Gift For You

Apart from that, I'll also send you Announcements of my New Releases and Promos.

I won't send you anything that's not related to my stories and I won't share your information with any person or entity.

CLICK TO READ FOR FREE

or Copy this Link -> stats.sender.net/ forms/er756a/view

Note: Please check your Spam or Promotions tab
if the confirmation doesn't arrive in your inbox.

Love Always, Lilly

Chapter 1

∞∞∞

I T WAS ONE OF THOSE NEW YORK AFTERNOONS where the sun hung low in the sky, casting a golden hue on the city. The smell of exhaust and hot dog vendors wafted in from the open door, fighting for dominance with the sour tang of stale beer.

The Corner Pocket, a local sports bar off the beaten path, was my chosen refuge from the monotony of Ivy League academia.

My buddies, Marco and Vinny, were already deep into their own pitchers when I arrived. Marco wore a well-loved Yankees cap, sweat stains blossoming around the brim. He was a bear of a man, broad-shouldered with dark eyes that belied an intellect few expected from his rough exterior.

Vinny, on the other hand, was as wiry as Marco was bulky. His darting eyes hid beneath a mop of curly hair, his every movement punctuated by the clink of his studded leather bracelets.

I was half a dozen drinks in, my shirt—some ironic graphic tee I'd snagged off a clearance rack —sticking to my back in the summer heat. My jeans, worn at the knees from too many late-night adventures, hugged my lanky frame as I slumped over the bar counter.

"Watch this, guys," I slurred, jabbing my finger at the TV screen where Lisa, Columbia University's reigning beauty queen and the object of every straight man's fantasy, was being interviewed by some campus news channel.

I could almost taste the minty lip gloss she always wore, my mind wandering back to that one Halloween party last year. Her eyes, as blue as an afternoon sky, shone with something akin to intrigue whenever we crossed paths.

"I'll have her eating out of the palm of my hand by the end of the week," I boasted. The declaration was bold, but not entirely ungrounded. My looks had always been my trump card. Tall, blonde, a little too pretty for my own good—attributes that had served me well throughout high school and beyond.

"Yeah right, Jim," Marco drawled, rolling his

eyes. He traced the rim of his glass, his fingertips leaving trails of condensation on the cold glass. Vinny merely snorted, flicking a peanut shell at me with a smirk.

The nickname 'pretty boy' was one I had acquired over the years. It was a moniker I wore like a badge, though I doubted it was meant as a compliment. Nonetheless, my feminine features hadn't hurt my prospects. The square jaw and prominent cheekbones that had earned me the title of prom king hadn't faded since high school.

There was something intoxicating about the bar atmosphere, something that wasn't solely down to the steady flow of alcohol. The musty scent of old carpeting, the smooth texture of the worn-out bar counter beneath my fingertips, the distant cheering of a football game on TV—all mingled together in a sensory cocktail that was as comforting as it was familiar.

There were times I'd catch a whiff of something—greasy fries or cheap cologne—and I'd be transported back to high school. Back to stolen beers, reckless dares, and the exhilaration of driving too fast down empty suburban streets.

The fabric of those memories was woven from the same cloth as these afternoons at Corner Pocket, their essence distilled in the chill of the beer that numbed my tongue and the way the sunrays fractured through the dirty bar windows.

"Seriously, Jim?" Vinny's voice cut through my haze of nostalgia, pulling me back to the present. His eyebrows were knitted in that familiar skeptical expression, but his eyes held a glimmer of amusement.

"Bet you twenty bucks you can't do it," Marco chimed in, the corners of his mouth twitching into a smirk. I could smell the stale beer on his breath as he leaned towards me, his challenge hanging in the air between us.

"You're on," I declared, extending my hand for him to shake. My words were laced with the confidence only a decent alcohol buzz can provide. I glanced back at the TV, Lisa's image replaced by some highlights from last night's game. The echoes of her laughter still played in my mind, a melody that held the promise of something more.

Moments later, Marco was the first to notice her. "Look," he said, his voice dropping to a conspiratorial whisper. The condensation-laden beer pitcher slid against the worn oak tabletop as he gestured towards the bar's grimy window.

A girl stood there, her petite frame cloaked in the classic navy blue and white uniform of Lady

Liberty University—an all-girls school a couple neighborhoods over.

She was pretty, with a mane of blonde hair that caught the golden sunlight and a pair of eyes that were enough to hypnotize anyone in her midst. Her book bag was slung over one shoulder, textbooks peeking out from the open flap, a sharp contrast to the frivolous laughter and beer-soaked ambiance inside the bar.

Vinny followed Marco's gaze and his eyebrows shot up, a wide grin splitting his face.

He nudged me, "Jim, you're up."

I raised an eyebrow, my attention now torn away from the sports reruns on the TV.

"What are you talking about?" I asked, though their amused faces said it all. It was a dare, another opportunity to showcase my charms, even though I was still smarting from the last time.

They wanted me to get her number. Drunk as I was, I couldn't resist the challenge. An impulsive nod sealed my fate, my friends' cheering drowned out by the throbbing pulse in my ears.

Shoving off the barstool, I straightened out

my graphic tee, and pushed a hand through my tousled blonde hair, hoping it looked more 'devil-may-care' than 'bedraggled'. The cool metal of the door handle was a stark contrast to the warm, hazy air inside.

The first thing that hit me was the buzz of the city. Car horns blaring in the distance, the smell of exhaust fumes mixed with the savory aroma of a nearby food stand. The sidewalk beneath my worn-out sneakers was gritty, the reality outside a stark contrast to the beer-bubble we had been living in inside the bar.

I approached her with the swagger that had won me more numbers than I could count. Cocky, sure, but this was a game to me, one that I was usually pretty damn good at.

"Hey, sweetheart," I drawled, plastering a confident smile on my face as I caressed her lower back.

"I think you dropped something." I waved my phone in front of her, my number screen glowing against the dying sunlight—my fingers, sinking to her waist like we had known each other for a long time. It was a line that had served me well in the past.

She looked up from her phone, her eyes, a bright green, met mine. She studied me for a moment before a slow smile curved her lips.

"Yeah, you're right. You also dropped something, *sweetheart*," she said.

There was something in that smile, something that said she saw right through me.

"Here you go," she continued.

She reached up, her fingers brushing my cheek lightly before a resounding slap echoed down the street.

I stood there, stunned, as she turned to board the bus that had conveniently pulled up. She then tossed me a saucy salute, the universal sign for 'flip off', before disappearing into the belly of the city bus.

The roar of laughter from inside the bar reached my ears before I even stepped back inside, my cheeks still burning from the surprise slap. Marco and Vinny were practically rolling on the floor, their mirth so strong it shook the wooden table. The taste of failure was more bitter than any beer I'd ever drunk.

"Well, that didn't go as planned," I muttered to myself, running a hand through my hair. My usual smooth approach had been turned upside down by a petite blonde in a schoolgirl uniform. The irony wasn't lost on me.

But despite my bruised ego and stinging cheek, I couldn't help but laugh. The absurdity of it all, the unexpected twist, was what made these days memorable. Back inside, the bar was exactly as I left it—my beer still cold, the TV still playing sports reruns, and my friends, Marco and Vinny, still laughing their asses off.

Sitting back down on my barstool, I shook my head and raised my beer for a toast.

"To being shot down," I declared, the echoes of laughter and clinking of glasses punctuating the end of another wild day. With each passing second, the sting of the slap faded, but the memory remained, etched into the rich tapestry of my college days, another wild tale to add to my 'Pretty Boy' legacy.

The shrill ring of my phone cut through the lingering laughter like a hot knife through butter. Marco and Vinny fell silent as I pulled my phone out of my pocket, squinting at the caller ID. Mom. I sighed, my cocky demeanor evaporating as quickly as it had come.

With an apologetic shrug to my friends, I

stepped out of the cacophony of the bar, pushing open the door to the quieter, but no less busy, street. The screen of my phone felt slick against my fingertips as I swiped to answer, bringing the device to my ear.

"Hi, Mom," I greeted, leaning against the cool brick wall of the bar. I closed my eyes against the afternoon sun, its fading warmth still a sharp contrast to the cool, conditioned air of the bar.

"Jim Forrest," my mother's voice crackled over the line, sharp like a whip, her tone that particular mix of disappointment and worry that only moms seemed to master.

"Where were you today!? You were supposed to meet Mrs. Wortham for lunch!"

Mrs. Wortham. A friend from my mother's college days and a successful businesswoman with a bunch of connections that my mother believed would help me with my finals and an upcoming pitch deck for my marketing class.

"I...uh..." I stammered, running a hand through my hair. The smell of alcohol and bar food clung to my clothes, a telltale sign of my afternoon escapades. I glanced back at the bar, its neon signs beginning to glow in the dwindling daylight.

"All the buses to Manhattan were full," I lied, wincing at how pathetic it sounded even to my ears. The faint sound of traffic hummed in the background, the rush of tires on the asphalt, the occasional honking—all familiar sounds that felt somehow louder over the phone call.

A sigh sounded on the other end of the line.

"Jim, you need to take these things more seriously. You can't just squander your opportunities like this." Her voice was softer now, laced with that concern that had been a constant backdrop of my childhood.

I closed my eyes, her words stinging more than I cared to admit. The din of the city seemed to fade into the background, replaced by the sound of my mother's worry, and beneath it, her unyielding belief in my potential.

"I'm sorry, Mom," I mumbled, the words tasting of regret and the bitterness of wasted opportunities. The noise of the bar had been replaced by the quieter, yet somehow more profound, sounds of the city.

The distant blaring of car horns, the hushed murmur of people passing by, the soft rustling of trees lining the sidewalk—they all seemed to echo my remorse.

"I want you home, Jim," she said, her voice steady and sure. "We need to talk about this."

The call ended with a click, leaving behind a silence that was somehow louder than the noise of the city.

Chapter 2

∞∞∞

THE SHRILL RING OF MY PHONE FELL SILENT, leaving behind the noise of the cityscape and the steady beat of my heartbeat in my ears. I hesitated, thumb still hovering over the screen, as the weight of my mother's words settled around me.

Pushing off from the cool brick wall, I pocketed my phone and pushed open the door to the bar, the chill of the evening replaced by the warm, stuffy air inside. The murmur of conversation washed over me, accompanied by the faint clatter of glasses and the lingering scent of beer.

Marco and Vinny were still at our table, huddled over something on Marco's phone. The sight of them, so at ease and unburdened, was a stark contrast to the turmoil brewing within me. Yet as they looked up at my return, their faces splitting into wide grins, I felt a tug of familiarity that was hard to resist.

"There you are!" Marco exclaimed, waving me over.

"We're going to hit the Internet cafe next." He was already getting up, pushing his chair back with a loud screech that cut through the bar chatter.

I hesitated, torn between the lure of camaraderie and my mother's stern command. The Internet cafe—a haven of laughter, friendly competition, and mindless games—was a temptation I always found hard to resist.

Marco and Vinny were already heading towards the door, their laughter echoing off the wooden paneling and worn-out carpet.

"Come on, Jim!" Vinny called out, his voice tinged with that carefree excitement that seemed to be a part of him. He was already in his worn-out leather jacket, the one he claimed was his lucky charm for every game.

Despite the heavy feeling in my gut, I found myself following them. My mind screamed at me to go home, to be responsible. But my heart, it wanted to hold onto the remaining fragments of a carefree afternoon, even if just for a little while longer.

We made our way to the Internet cafe, a small establishment nestled between a pawnshop and a diner. Its neon sign buzzed, casting an eerie glow onto the sidewalk.

Inside, it was a different world. The hum of computers, the faint clicking of keyboards, and hushed voices created a soundscape that was both familiar and comforting.

We settled into our usual corner, the worn-out chairs and aged computers a testament to the countless hours we'd spent here. I logged into my account, the glow of the computer screen chasing away the thoughts of my looming conversation with my mother.

As the game loaded, I looked around. Vinny was already engrossed in his game, his face lit by the blueish light of the screen. Marco was chatting with the cafe owner, his laughter ringing out over the muted sounds of the cafe.

I found myself drawn into the game, the familiar graphics and gameplay offering a refuge from the real world. The worries of college, of my future, seemed to fade away as I navigated through digital battles, my only concern being the next quest, the next level.

Time lost its meaning as we played, the outside world reduced to a distant blur. The familiar sounds of the game, the soft click of the mouse, the hushed strategy discussions with Marco and Vinny filled my senses, drowning out the gnawing guilt at the back of my mind.

As I emerged from the digital world hours later, the real world rushed back at me. The cafe had emptied out, the only sound being the hum of the computers and the occasional clink from the cafe counter. The smell of stale coffee lingered in the air, a stark contrast to the crisp evening air sneaking in through the slightly ajar door.

Marco and Vinny were still engrossed in their game, oblivious to the passage of time. I glanced at my phone, the screen lighting up to reveal several missed calls from home. The weight of the impending confrontation settled around me, heavier than before.

As I said my goodbyes and stepped out of the cafe, the city seemed quieter, more subdued. The usual symphony of sounds was replaced by the occasional car passing by, the city slowly succumbing to the late-night silence.

The houses in our corner of Queens were all tucked together like books on a shelf, their exteriors muted under the dim glow of the streetlights.

As I pushed open the door to our home, the familiar sight was tinged with an uncomfortable sense of dread.

With every step towards the front door, the knot in my stomach tightened, the shadows cast by the porch light elongating my guilt on the cobblestones below. The lights in the living room shone brightly through the blinds, the silent indicator that my parents were still up, waiting.

Pushing open the door, I stepped into the familiar chaos that was home. The aroma of dinner long finished still lingered in the air, a sad reminder of another missed family meal.

The ticking of the wall clock, the hum of the refrigerator, the soft glow of the television—they were all wrapped in an uncomfortable shroud of anticipation.

And then, like a match thrown into a pile of dry leaves, my mom appeared. She was in her worn-out nightgown, her hair tied up in a messy bun, and her face a mask of worry and frustration. She was a petite woman, her fiery personality completely at odds with her small frame. The moment she saw me, her features morphed into a picture of disappointment.

"Jim Forrest!" Her voice sliced through the room, making me wince. She always used my full name when she was upset, each syllable echoing with the weight of her disappointment.

"Where have you been? Do you have any idea what time it is?"

"I..." I started, my voice barely above a whisper, but she wasn't in the mood for explanations.

"Do you think this is some kind of a joke?!" She cut me off, her hands on her hips, her eyes sharp like two laser points.

"Your father and I have spent our entire life savings to give you a chance, a future!"

As she unleashed her tirade, I could do nothing but stand there, taking it all in. Her words, laced with hurt and frustration, crashed around the room, their echoes serving as a harsh reminder of my actions. I could smell her worry, feel her disappointment, taste the regret in the air.

"And what do you do?!" She continued, not waiting for an answer.

"You skip classes, spend the night playing those ridiculous games, come home smelling like liquor at ungodly hours!"

I made my way to my room, her words

following me like a dark cloud. The well-worn carpet under my feet, the familiar layout of the hallway, the faint humming of the air conditioner —they were all a stark contrast to the chaos brewing behind me.

As I pushed open the door to my room and closed it behind me, the muffled sounds of my mom's tirade broke through the silence. My room, usually a haven of peace, was now tainted with the same guilt and regret that seemed to have taken hold of the rest of the house.

As I kicked off my shoes and sank onto my bed, the comfort of the soft mattress did little to ease the tension. My room, filled with posters of my favorite bands, the cluttered desk littered with textbooks, the well-worn gaming console—they all bore silent witness to my shame.

My mom's voice, though muffled by the closed door, was still as potent as ever. Her words, sharp and punctuated by years of sacrifice and hope, stabbed at my conscience, each one a glaring reminder of my actions.

"You're throwing away your future!" Her voice pierced through the wooden door.

"Is this how you repay us!?"

I laid there, her words bouncing off the walls

of my room, the guilt seeping into every corner, every crevice. As I closed my eyes, the familiar scent of my room was replaced by the bitter smell of regret.

The soft hum of the air conditioner was drowned out by the echoes of my mom's words.

As the night crept on, I found myself wide awake, my mother's voice ringing in my ears, the weight of my actions pressing down on me.

Chapter 3

∞∞∞

THREE DAYS LATER, I found myself in the middle of a lecture on the intricacies of management strategies. The steady hum of the professor's voice was drowned out by my own whirlpool of thoughts.

The classroom was a melting pot of students from various walks of life, each with their own dreams and aspirations, all somehow managing to find a connection with the course. I, on the other hand, felt like a fish out of water, my interest in business management as deep as a puddle on a sunny day.

I was seated in the back of the lecture hall, the drone of the professor's voice lulling me into a state of mindless stupor. The words were a jumble, the concepts a blur, my notes an abstract representation of my confusion.

The scent of the musty lecture hall, the sharp scratch of pens on paper, the faint chatter from the back rows—they were all background noise in the symphony of my boredom.

My mind began to wander, drifting away from the mind-numbing jargon of business management to that unexpected encounter a few days back. The image of the blonde girl in her uniform sprang up unbidden, her amused smile followed by the stinging slap, her laughter as she flipped me off before boarding the bus.

She was like a breath of fresh air, a spark of unpredictability in my predictable world. The memory of her smell, a mix of soft perfume and the faint musky scent of city life, lingered in my mind. Her voice, although I had only heard a few words, was clear and sharp, cutting through my drunken stupor with ease.

I recalled the way her eyes sparkled with mischief before she slapped me, the way her laughter filled the air. The sting of the slap, the shocked silence that followed, the roar of the bus as it pulled away—they were all ingrained in my memory, a stark reminder of my cocky foolishness.

I could still feel the sting of the slap, a ghostly

sensation that came back every time I thought of her. The way she carried herself, the confidence in her voice, the spark in her eyes—they were all in stark contrast to the blandness of my college life.

I cringed as the embarrassment washed over me, a wave of mortification that made me sink further into my chair. The memory of my friends' laughter echoed in my ears, a haunting soundtrack to my embarrassment. The taste of defeat still lingered, a bitter pill that was hard to swallow.

But amidst the embarrassment, there was also a faint admiration for her. She stood up to me, didn't fall for my drunken charm, didn't get swayed by my pretty boy looks.

She was real, raw, and refreshingly unpredictable.

After class, I met Marco and Vinny outside the lecture hall, a familiar trio in the sea of exiting students. Marco, in his usual vintage band t-shirt and worn-out jeans, was laughing about something Vinny had said.

Vinny, on the other hand, was dressed in a crisp white button-down shirt and tailored pants, looking more like he was ready for a business meeting than a casual catch-up.

"Jimbo!" Vinny called out, a wide grin plastered across his face. His eyes were sparkling with excitement, a clear indication that he had some good news to share. Marco playfully elbowed him, a smirk on his face.

"Guess what, man? It's my birthday and drinks are on me," Vinny announced, an offer as tempting as an oasis in a desert.

"We're heading to this new club downtown. Heard it's swarming with college girls, even Lisa's been spotted there."

My heart jumped at the mention of Lisa's name. Lisa, the university's unofficial queen bee, was the epitome of beauty and grace, a woman who could make any guy swoon with just a glance.

My guilt about skipping classes and the lingering sting of the slap momentarily forgotten, I was swept away by the anticipation of a night filled with laughter, booze, and maybe, just maybe, a chance encounter with Lisa.

As we walked towards the parking lot, Vinny's chatter filled the air, his excitement contagious. The prospect of a night out, a chance to escape the boredom of college life, was a welcome distraction.

The sound of laughter, the clink of glasses, the pulsating music, the smell of alcohol mixed with the sweet perfume of women—they all seemed tantalizingly within reach.

I found myself chuckling at the thought of the impending night. My conscience, that little nagging voice at the back of my head, was conveniently silenced by the tantalizing prospect of an unforgettable night. The mundane worries of college life, the looming deadlines, the unending lectures, they all seemed insignificant compared to the lure of a wild night out.

Marco, ever the joker, began mimicking Lisa's high-pitched voice and her signature hair flip, sending us into fits of laughter. Vinny, with his impeccable timing, pretended to swoon, adding fuel to our laughter. The world around us, with its hustle and bustle, faded into the background as we surrendered to the infectious laughter.

We hopped into Vinny's old, beaten-up Chevy, its rusty exterior a stark contrast to the sleek, modern cars around us. The smell of worn-out leather seats, the faint hum of the engine, the soft murmur of the radio—they all added to the atmosphere of anticipation.

Just as I settled into the worn-out leather of the Chevy, a hint of rebellious grin played on

Marco's lips.

"Why don't we head to the gaming café first?" he suggested, eyes glinting with an idea.

"The club won't open till 9."

The proposal didn't come as a surprise; the café was our hideout, our sanctuary from the overwhelming course load and the mundane college life. Sitting in dimly lit corners, absorbed in our fantasy worlds on screen, we found solace, we found freedom. Plus, the opportunity to kill time before the night truly came alive was too good to pass up.

Then it was time to hit the club.

We drove under a sky ablaze with stars, the city lights dancing in a symphony of colors. The excitement was high, the night young, and the possibilities endless. The bass pounding in the distance was the siren song pulling us closer, the neon sign of the club a beacon guiding our way.

Walking into the club was like stepping into a vortex of pulsating energy. The music was deafening, a rhythmic drumbeat in sync with our racing hearts. The lights, the haze, the perfume-laden air, the animated chatter, the electrifying atmosphere—everything was intoxicating. The sight of young bodies moving in rhythm, the sensation of the thumping bass under my feet, the tantalizing scent of cocktails and heady perfumes —it was a sensory overload.

We scored a table near the dance floor, a perfect vantage point to scan the crowd. The drinks arrived, a colorful parade of temptation. The bitter-sweet taste of beer, the bite of tequila, the tangy sweetness of cocktails. Every sip was a promise of a night to remember.

As the hours melted away, so did our inhibitions. We danced with girls we had never met before, laughing, flirting, living in the moment.

The soft touch of a girl's hand in mine, the sight of her smile, the scent of her perfume, the whisper of her laughter in my ear—it was all part of the night's intoxicating charm.

Then, around 11 PM, she arrived. Lisa, the goddess among mortals, swept in with her posse. The sight of her, bathed in the club's neon glow, was enough to make my heart race. With newfound courage, fueled by alcohol and adrenaline, I asked her to dance.

Her response was a teasing smile and a playful, "Yes, pretty boy." Dancing with Lisa was like living a dream. The feel of her hand in mine, the sight of her radiant smile, the intoxicating scent of her perfume, the rhythm of our bodies swaying in sync—it was a dance of attraction, a dance of desire.

By 1 AM, I was drunk, the world spinning around me in a blur of colors and sounds. The noise of the club, the bright lights, the taste of alcohol on my tongue, the sensation of the pulsating music, the sight of Lisa dancing—everything felt surreal, distant.

A buzz in my pocket jerked me back to reality. It was a series of text messages from my mom, each one growing more frantic. My heart sank at the sight of the messages, the worry creeping back in.

I wished Vinny a happy birthday again, a sense of melancholy creeping in. My friends, my night, my escape—it was all coming to an end. The laughter, the music, the lights, the smell of alcohol—everything felt different, tinged with an impending goodbye.

With a heavy heart, I decided to take the subway home. The night was ending, the dream was fading. The club, with its bright lights and intoxicating atmosphere, receded in the background. The journey home was a solitary one, a stark contrast to the wild, vibrant night.

Descending the stairs of the subway station, I was greeted by a sight I didn't expect to see. There she was, the same blonde college girl from Lady Liberty University I'd encountered outside the bar days ago.

She stood near the edge of the platform, a vibrant blue headband holding her golden locks in place. In the grim, gray station, she was an anomaly-a splash of color, a burst of life.

She teetered on the platform, too close to the edge, playfully chanting, "I can fly, I can fly." Her words echoed in the cavernous expanse, colliding with the sound of the subway train's ominous roar in the distance.

A chill ran down my spine; something was amiss. It was an unsettling sight.

The echo of her voice, the sight of her swaying dangerously near the edge, the smell of damp concrete and the lingering scent of her sweet perfume, the cold metallic touch of the handrails —everything was heightened, the danger palpable.

The subway station was deserted, it was just her and me, and the distant rumble of the approaching train. The bright fluorescent lights of the station cast long, ominous shadows on the platform, creating a haunting, surreal scene.

The contrast of her colorful uniform against the drab gray surroundings, the stark fear reflected in her seemingly innocent playfulness, it all made for a chilling tableau.

As the sound of the train got louder, so did my heartbeat. The adrenaline started pumping through my veins, erasing any trace of my drunken stupor.

The sweet, overpowering taste of fear mixed with the stale air of the subway station. The bright lights, the increasing noise, the chill of the metallic rails under my fingertips, the faint scent of rust—the impending danger heightened my senses.

In a flash, I was moving toward her. Every step felt heavy, yet I was running, propelled by an urgency I didn't know I possessed.

The cold wind was slapping against my face, the sound of my frantic steps echoed in my ears, the taste of fear lingered in my mouth— everything else blurred as I focused solely on the girl swaying dangerously at the edge of the platform.

Time seemed to slow down. The sight of the subway lights, the deafening sound of the train, the chilly wind against my face, the sharp taste of fear—everything faded into the background as I pushed her out of the way, my arms wrapping around her small frame just in time.

The train whooshed past us, the gust of wind it brought with it whipping through my hair, its deafening roar echoing in my ears.

In the aftermath of the terrifying ordeal, the station was eerily quiet. All I could hear was the sound of our heavy breathing, the steady beat of my heart reverberating in my chest. The cold concrete under us, the distant hum of the train fading away, the scent of her perfume mixed with fear—it was an overwhelming sensory overload.

With her safely in my arms, I took a moment to gather my bearings.

My heart was still racing, my hands shaking from the adrenaline rush. The feel of her against me, the scent of her hair, the sight of her closed eyes—it was a surreal moment, a horrifyingly beautiful scene etched in my mind.

Then, to my surprise, she murmured two words, "So pretty."

Her fingers grazed my face, her touch sending shivers down my spine. Her voice was soft, her touch delicate—in contrast to the harsh, terrifying reality we had just escaped.

As her eyes fluttered shut, she slumped against me, her body going limp. The sight of her peaceful face, the feel of her body relaxing against mine, the soft scent of her perfume—it all felt strangely intimate, in stark contrast to the chaos that had just ensued.

Carrying her in my arms, I found a nearby bench and carefully set her down. The feel of the cold, metal bench beneath us, the lingering scent of fear and adrenaline, the soft whirring of the subway station's ventilation system—it was a startling return to reality.

"Hey," I said, but she was heavily drunk to hear me.

In the quiet station, as the minutes trickled by, I found myself lost in thoughts. The sight of her peaceful face, the feel of her breath against my skin, the scent of her hair—they were all reminders of the horrifying ordeal we had just been through, the near-death experience forever etching this night into my memory.

Chapter 4

∞∞∞

THE PEACEFUL SILENCE was abruptly shattered by the shrill buzz of my phone. I flinched, my heart pounding in my chest as I pulled it out. A string of text messages from Mom.

She was worried, angry, confused—all the emotions conveyed through a screen. The faint, almost metallic smell of the phone, the relentless buzzing against my palm, the bright glare of the screen in the dimly lit station—it all served as a harsh reminder of my responsibilities, my reality.

I glanced down at the girl asleep in my lap, her face serene. I felt a pang of guilt, a nagging sense of duty. I knew I had to get home, but I couldn't leave her there, alone and vulnerable.

The sight of her peaceful face, the steady rhythm of her breathing, the faint scent of her perfume—it made the decision harder, my conscience wouldn't let me walk away.

With a sigh of resignation, I gently nudged her, trying to rouse her from her deep slumber. Her only response was a soft murmur, a tiny frown marring her otherwise tranquil face.

The gentle touch of her skin, the warmth radiating from her, the sight of her frown—it only added to my guilt, my frustration.

Annoyance flared within me, replacing the guilt momentarily. I couldn't leave her there, but I also couldn't wake her up. The buzzing of my phone, the cool touch of the bench, the lingering scent of the subway—I felt trapped, my options limited.

With a final resigned sigh, I made a decision. I gingerly lifted her, her weight surprisingly light against my chest. As I stood there, with the sleeping girl on my back, I hastily looked for a nearby motel using my phone.

Navigating through the quiet, empty streets with the girl on my back was an ordeal in itself.

The distant sound of the city, the chill of the night air against my skin, the taste of fear and worry— it was an eerie journey, a solitary trek through the sleeping city that was supposed to never sleep.

When I finally reached the motel, the neon sign flickering in the cold night was a welcome sight. The harsh, buzzing sound of the sign, the cold touch of the doorknob, the stale smell of the motel lobby—it was a relief, a strange sanctuary from the haunting emptiness of the night.

The receptionist, a middle-aged man with a playful smile, looked us over, his eyes lingering on the sleeping girl.

"Wow, she's pretty. You're a lucky man," he commented, his tone teasing. The sight of his smug smile, the sound of his condescending words, the musty smell of the reception area—it all grated on my already frayed nerves.

"What the fuck," I muttered under my breath, feeling my cheeks flush in irritation. The harsh fluorescent light overhead, the cold countertop under my fingers, the stale taste in my mouth— I felt my patience wearing thin, my exhaustion taking over.

"Just give me the damn key," I said, my voice more harsh than I intended. The sharp sound of my words, the cold glare in the receptionist's eyes, the metallic jingle of keys—it was a sharp contrast to the serene silence of the subway station, the peaceful scene I had left behind.

With the key in my hand and the sleeping girl on my back, I trudged towards our room, the heavy door closing behind me with a final, resounding thud.

The faint smell of cleaning agents, the muted colors of the decor, the soft hum of the air conditioning—it was a stark shift from the grimy subway station, a strange sanctuary in the midst of the chaos.

I watched her as she slept, her chest rising and falling in a slow, steady rhythm. Her long, dark lashes fanned out against her pale skin, her lips slightly parted. An unwanted thought slipped into my mind, a spark of desire partnered with physical arousal.

Almost as if on cue, she stirred, her eyes fluttering open to meet mine. Her gaze was hazy, disoriented, but there was a spark there, a hint of recognition. The sight of her sleepy eyes, the faint blush on her cheeks, the warm scent of her skin—it was seductive, tempting.

She leaned in, her intent clear. My heart pounded in my chest, the room suddenly feeling too warm. But just as I was bracing myself for the kiss, she recoiled, a hand clamped over her mouth. The sight of her paling face, the sound of her retching, the acidic smell of vomit—it was jarring, a harsh contrast to the romantic tension moments ago.

"What the hell?!" I muttered, staring at her in disbelief. The cold touch of the motel's tiled floor, the sour smell lingering in the room, the harsh echo of my words—it all served to snap me back to reality, my fleeting moment of desire swiftly replaced by disgust.

She stumbled towards the bathroom, the sound of her heaving echoing through the room. After what felt like an eternity, she emerged from the bathroom, a weak smile on her face. The sight of her drained face, the sound of her labored breathing, the faint hint of mint—it was all so painfully human, a stark contrast to the divine image I'd painted in my mind earlier.

Without another word, she curled up on the bed, her breathing evening out as she fell back into a deep slumber. The sight of her peaceful face, the soft sound of her breathing, the comforting warmth radiating from her—it felt almost surreal, a bizarre end to a long, exhausting night.

With a weary sigh, I decided to clean up, the

warm spray of the shower washing away the grime and fatigue. The rhythmic sound of the water, the steamy warmth enveloping me, the sharp scent of soap—it was a moment of solace, a fleeting escape from the chaos outside.

After I was done, I called the receptionist, requesting a lady caretaker to help wash her clothes. The sound of the phone ringing, the cold touch of the receiver, the sharp scent of my freshly washed skin—it was a necessary step, a painful reminder of the predicament I had landed myself in.

I returned to the room just as the caretaker was leaving, a brief nod of acknowledgment passing between us. With that done, I decided to head back home, the night's events playing on a loop in my mind.

The cool night air against my skin, the distant hum of the city, the faint taste of regret—it was a quiet cab ride, a solitary journey through the sleeping city.

As expected, Mom was waiting for me, a tirade ready to be unleashed. The sound of her raised voice, the cold glare in her eyes, the faint scent of worry—it was a harsh welcome, a stark contrast to the relative peace of the motel room.

Despite her words, my thoughts kept drifting back to the girl. The sight of her sleeping face, the soft sound of her laughter, the warm scent of her skin—it was haunting, etching itself into my memories.

But intertwined with it was the harsh reality —the sound of her retching, the sour smell of vomit, the cold touch of the bathroom tiles. It was a strange mix of attraction and repulsion, a confusing whirlpool of emotions.

As I lay in bed, Mom's words fading into a distant hum, I found myself thinking about the girl. The sight of her sleepy smile, the soft sound of her breathing, the faint hint of her perfume— it was strangely soothing, a fleeting moment of peace amid the chaos of my life. The memory of her, as disturbing as it was endearing, drowned out Mom's nagging, lulling me into a restful sleep.

Chapter 5

∞ ∞ ∞

STANDING BEFORE THE GRAND ARCHWAY of my university, I fumbled around my pockets for my ID, cursing under my breath. The touch of my frayed denim jeans, the scent of damp concrete around, the sight of the busy campus—all of it felt too real, too normal for the whirlwind of a night I'd just lived.

"Where the fuck is it?" I muttered, growing increasingly frustrated. The sharp tang of unease was now prickling on my tongue, the taste of an impending disaster.

Suddenly, my phone rang, the harsh, jarring sound cutting through my thoughts.

"Meet me at McDonald's now!" came a voice from the other end, instantly setting off alarm bells in my head. It was her voice, sharp, cold, and strangely sober. The smell of her perfume and the softness of her skin were still fresh in my memory, stirring up a cocktail of emotions.

"Who's this?" I played dumb, trying to buy some time. The cool morning breeze was biting at my skin, the smell of fresh coffee from the nearby cafeteria wafting in the air, the murmur of bustling students was growing louder —everything was so typical, so ordinary for the bomb she just dropped.

"I'm the girl you took advantage of!" she spat, her words like ice daggers. The sour taste of guilt rose in my throat, the sound of her voice echoing in my ears. I wanted to explain, but my mind was a mess, my thoughts tangled.

"What? No! That's not how it happened," I stammered out, my words falling on deaf ears. The scent of morning dew, the sound of chattering students, the sight of the sun shining overhead – everything felt hazy, distorted under the weight of her accusation.

"Which McDonald's?" I finally managed to ask, my words barely a whisper.

"I'll send you my location," she declared before hanging up, leaving me standing there, staring at my phone. The morning air felt colder, the sound of students walking by seemed muted, the taste of my own uncertainty lingered—the regular world was continuing while mine had just imploded.

Guilt, confusion, and regret swirled within me as I made my way to McDonald's, my mind replaying the events of the previous night. The slick feel of the subway pole, the sweet scent of her hair, the taste of fear as I pulled her back from the edge—it all came rushing back, clouding my senses.

The cold air brushed against my face as I walked, the sounds of the bustling city only adding to the cacophony in my head. The sight of everyday life playing out around me felt surreal, the tastes and smells of the city starkly contrasting my inner turmoil.

By the time I arrived at McDonald's, my heart was pounding in my chest, a rhythmic drum echoing my unease. The sight of the golden arches, the smell of fried food, the buzz of conversation around me—it all felt disconnected, disjointed from the nightmare I was living.

"Deep breaths, Jim," I whispered to myself, forcing down the lump of anxiety in my throat. The chilled air of the restaurant, the tang of fast food on my tongue, the soft hum of the overhead lights – it was oddly grounding, a semblance of normalcy amidst the chaos.

There she was, standing in a corner, her arms crossed over her chest. She was still wearing the Lady Liberty University all-girls school uniform —the soft, powder-blue material catching the afternoon sunlight, the gold emblem gleaming. The sight of it was oddly comforting in all the chaos.

"Sit down!" she commanded, pointing to the chair opposite her. I could smell the faint scent of her perfume—a mix of sweet apples and spring flowers—as I moved to comply. The sound of her voice was no longer cold, but the sharp edge of authority still cut through the air.

Clearing my throat, I began to gingerly explain what had happened the previous night. My words painted a picture—the screech of the subway, the metallic smell, the cold, hard platform.

The memory was vivid, awakening all my senses.

As I explained about the motel and my decision to request a female caretaker to help her change, she sat in silence. Her eyes, as deep and blue as the uniform she wore, stared at me without blinking.

The tension in the air tasted bitter, like a gulp of black coffee on an empty stomach.

Suddenly, her lips curled into a smile, her eyes warming up.

"Okay, good," she said, her voice losing its frosty edge. The unexpected reaction threw me off, the scent of her relief mixing with the fast-food air, creating an oddly intoxicating aroma.

Then, she extended her hand to me, my student ID in her grasp. The sight of the familiar plastic card, the feel of my own embossed name under my fingertips, it all brought a sense of normalcy rushing back.

"I like apple pie and fries," she casually declared, her statement hanging in the air. The thought of the sweet pie and salty fries made my mouth water, the juxtaposition of tastes mirroring the roller coaster of emotions I was experiencing.

Wordlessly, I rose to order, my boots echoing against the tiled floor.

Opting for a Big Mac, I was about to confirm my order when I felt a tap on my shoulder. Whirling around, I met her piercing gaze.

"Order the same," she demanded, her voice stern. I quickly amended my order, the taste of the upcoming meal already dancing on my tongue.

As we started eating, she began to ask me questions—about who I was, my hobbies, my favorite music.

"Dogs or cats?"

I shook my head as I didn't like either, "I don't have pets."

She looked at me with disgust and said, "How

could you be so soulless?"

It felt like a first date, but the circumstances were far from typical. As I answered her queries, my mind was a whirlpool of thoughts, 'Wow, she's insane!' being the prominent one.

"I'm so thirsty, let's go to Marty's," she suddenly suggested. I almost choked on my fries at the abrupt change of plans, the strong taste of salt lingering on my tongue.

Marty's, a sports bar notorious for its cheap drinks, was the last place I expected her to suggest. The thought of going there with her was a mix of surprise and curiosity—much like the smell of rain on a sunny day, unexpected yet intriguing.

Leaving behind the smell of frying oil and the hum of the fast-food joint, we stepped out into the bustling city. The world seemed to be a cacophony of sounds, sights, smells, and tastes, each sensation blending into the next.

As I followed her to Marty's, I could still taste the apple pie on my tongue, the sweetness of the memory of our unconventional breakfast lingering.

There we were, ensconced in the corner of

Marty's, a haven of sticky tabletops and neon signs. The air was heavy with the smell of stale beer and musky cologne, the aroma curling around me like smoke.

"No, he wants whiskey shots," she told the waiter, her voice slicing through the din of clinking bottles and muffled conversations. I could only gape, my intentions of savoring a slow beer obliterated by her audacious declaration.

As the waiter left to fulfill the daring order, she resumed her inquisition.

"If you had to choose between being invisible or being able to fly, which one would you pick?" she asked, her eyes twinkling with an inscrutable mischief.

"Flying, I guess," I replied, intrigued by her whimsical line of questioning.

"Ah! An adventurer," she concluded, her eyes gleaming with what felt like approval.

Our shots arrived, amber liquid swirling in the small glasses. The strong scent of whiskey wafted up, stinging my nostrils. I took a deep breath, feeling the anticipation buzz through my veins like electricity.

After the first shot, the room seemed to take on a warm glow, the second made the noise around us recede to a low hum, and by the third, I felt the hard edge of reality soften.

That's when we heard it—the rough, derogatory voices from the adjacent table.

"Don't you know your date's a dude?" The harsh words hit me like a physical blow, the malice in the tone unmistakable. Turning to the source, I saw a group of men harassing a transgender woman who was on a date. The smile on her face had frozen into a pained grimace, her discomfort palpable.

Before I could react, she was on her feet, her face a mask of righteous fury. The sight was stunning, like witnessing a storm brewing at sea.

"Hey!"

"Do you have any idea about the Equality Act?" she bellowed, her voice echoing across the bar.

"It's a federal law, you ignoramus. It prohibits discrimination based on gender identity and sexual orientation! Your harassment here is a federal offense!"

Her tirade was punctuated by the stunned silence that fell over the bar. The scent of fear wafted from the men, it was heady, intoxicating.

"You want me to beat you up!? Mind your own damn business!" she snapped, her threat hanging heavy in the air.

A shiver of fear coursed through me, but it was overshadowed by a surge of admiration. She was like a tempest—wild, fierce, and utterly fearless. Her bravery was awe-inspiring, an unshakable monument in the sea of uncertainty that was my life.

With that, she sat down, her storm having passed.

"Those fuckers," she muttered, her fingers

closing around her shot glass. The harsh gulp that followed, the determined set of her jaw, it all spoke volumes about her resilience.

And then, as if the switch had been flipped, she crumpled, her body sagging against the booth. The world fell into a surreal silence, the echo of her voice, the scent of her perfume, the feel of the cool glass in my hand—it all seemed to freeze as she passed out.

"Not again," I muttered under my breath, my heart thumping loudly in my chest.

Looking down at her sleeping form, I gingerly reached for her bag, its worn leather soft against my fingertips. As I dug into its contents, the scent of spearmint gum and old paper hit me. I turned the contents over, searching for any sort of ID or address. But there was none. It felt like peering into a mystery, one that I was rapidly becoming embroiled in.

Deciding my next course of action, I opted for the nearby motel with her on my back, familiar from our earlier escapade. The cool metal of my ID burned in my pocket, a silent reminder of the chaos that was my life these past few days.

The walk to the motel was a blur with her weight on my back and my mind swirling with thoughts, my senses taking in every detail.

The motel room was nondescript, the kind of place that drowned in its own mediocrity. The wallpaper, a faded rose pattern, seemed to flake off under my gaze. The scent of disinfectant mingled with a lingering mustiness, a futile attempt to mask the odors of countless past inhabitants.

I laid her gently on the bed, her hair fanning out on the faded pillowcase, the fabric rough under my touch.

With one last glance at her sleeping form, I slipped out of the motel room, the cheap carpet scratchy under my shoes. As I stepped out into the bustle of the city, I couldn't help but feel a sense of liberation, a momentary relief from the whirlwind that was her.

The subway ride to the university was mundane, a stark contrast to the craziness of the day. The usual cacophony of the city seemed to recede into a gentle hum, a soothing symphony that helped clear my head. The swaying of the subway, the rhythm of the city, it all melted into a comforting lull, a much-needed breather.

As I emerged onto the campus, the familiar surroundings grounded me, the smell of fresh-cut grass and old books welcoming me back.

I could see my classmates huddled in groups, their laughter cutting through the warm afternoon air. Their everyday normality felt jarring, my chaotic morning a stark contrast to their mundane day.

Stepping into the classroom, I felt a wave of relief wash over me. The sight of the whiteboard, the smell of chalk dust, the hum of the air conditioner—it was a piece of my old life, a slice of normality that I clung onto.

The classroom was like a sanctuary, a haven amidst the storm that was brewing outside.

As the professor droned on about theoretical physics, I couldn't help but let my mind wander back to her. My senses were filled with the remnants of our encounter—the lingering smell of her perfume, the sight of her crumpled in the booth, the feel of her warm body against mine, the taste of her chosen whiskey still lingering on my tongue.

It felt like a part of her had latched onto me, a shadow of her essence that followed me around.

My day passed in a blur, my mind a whirlpool of thoughts, my senses constantly seeking her out in the crowded corridors and noisy canteens. It felt like I was living two lives—one in the humdrum of college and another in the chaotic whirlwind that was her.

The sun dipped low in the sky, casting long shadows across the campus as I trudged back to the subway. My heart pounded in my chest, the approaching evening a reminder of the storm that awaited me.

As the city lights blinked to life, bathing the world in a warm glow, I couldn't help but feel an undercurrent of excitement ripple through me. She was like a captivating book, one that I couldn't put down, a puzzle I was eager to solve.

Chapter 6

∞∞∞

T HE NEXT MORNING, the vibration in my pocket startled me from a half-hearted attempt to focus on the lecture about marketing theories. I pulled my phone out, my thumb brushing over the screen to reveal her number.

An unfamiliar warmth spread in my chest as I read the message—she wanted to meet at a Subway restaurant nearby. A quick glance at the class clock told me it was only 11 AM, still an hour left for the lunch break. But there was no way I could focus now, not with her message burning a hole in my pocket.

I made up some excuse about feeling sick and hurried out of the class. The concrete beneath my shoes felt hard, each step reverberating through me. The university grounds were still quiet at this hour, only a few early lunch-goers milling about. The cool morning air whipped at my face as I hastened to the bus stop.

Arriving at the restaurant, the familiar sight of the green and yellow sign comforted me. The glass doors opened to a wave of warm, yeasty air that reminded me of fresh bread. The scent mingled with the tangy aroma of marinara sauce and the sharp, unmistakable smell of onions.

She was seated in a corner, her back turned to me. Her hair was pulled into a loose ponytail, a single strand falling to frame her face. As I approached, she turned to face me, her eyes soft, a stark contrast to the fire I'd seen in them the day before.

She stood up abruptly, her chair scraping against the tiled floor. The motion startled me, my hands momentarily freezing on the wrapper of my half-eaten sandwich. With a swift move that I didn't see coming, she engulfed me in a warm hug. It was an innocent act, yet something about it touched a chord within me.

The softness of her hair against my cheek, the faint smell of her shampoo—something fruity and exotic, the warmth radiating from her body, it all felt comforting.

She released me just as abruptly and walked towards the counter. I watched her, momentarily dazed by the unexpected gesture. She returned with a tray laden with a variety of sandwiches and drinks.

She then set the tray on the table, a small, apologetic smile playing on her lips.

"This is my apology gift," she said, gesturing towards the food. Her voice was a bit lower now, almost shy.

We ate mostly in silence. The taste of fresh lettuce and creamy mayo was soon replaced by a myriad of flavors as we dug into the sandwiches. The tang of the pickles, the smoky taste of the meat, the crispness of the bread, every bite was a delightful exploration of tastes.

Finally, she broke the silence, her voice cutting through the low hum of the restaurant.

"I'm sorry I hadn't introduced myself earlier, I'm Mandy." She extended her hand towards me, her gaze steady.

"And I already know your name so you don't have to introduce yourself."

There was a playful glint in her eyes as she spoke, but I felt a chill run down my spine. It wasn't fear, but an inexplicable feeling of vulnerability.

Before I could dwell on it, she changed the topic.

"I have a fun-filled day planned for us,

you should finish your meal quickly." Her voice was full of anticipation, her eyes shining with excitement.

I hesitated before answering.

"I have a class later," I said, my voice soft. Her smile dimmed a little, her eyes losing some of their spark.

"I see... I understand." She sighed, her shoulders sagging slightly.

Something in me felt a pang of guilt, but I pushed it away. It was then that I decided to confront her about her drinking habits. I gathered my thoughts, choosing my words carefully.

"If you can't handle your drink, you shouldn't be drinking at all. You always end up sleeping in public. It's dangerous," I blurted out, my words rushing out like a torrent.

I expected her to retaliate, to argue, to defend herself. But she didn't. She just nodded, her gaze dropping to her hands on the table. She was silent for a while before finally speaking, "You're right. I'll try to control it."

It was strange to see her so docile, so

subservient. I wasn't sure how to react, but I decided to continue. I lectured her on the dangers of drinking irresponsibly, the risks she was taking each time she passed out in a public place.

She listened to me attentively, nodding at appropriate times, her face serious.

The rest of the meal passed in silence. I felt a heavy tension between us, a weight that hung in the air. After finishing the sandwiches, I pushed back my chair and stood up.

"I have to go to my class," I told her, a bit awkwardly.

She smiled at me, a small, sad smile.

"Okay, see you later, Jim." Her voice was soft, almost a whisper. I felt a pang of guilt again but pushed it away.

"There's no later. I'll be busy the whole day." My words were harsher than I intended. She looked taken aback, her smile fading.

I left the restaurant, the taste of the sandwich still lingering in my mouth.

Back in the university, my mind was only half-focused on the professor's lecture about capital investments. He was a dry, monotone speaker, each sentence droning into the next. His words formed a background hum to the more interesting thoughts playing out in my head.

In spite of myself, my mind had become a screen playing endless reels of the morning's encounter with Mandy.

Suddenly, the door creaked open, a soft ray of sunlight slicing through the dimly lit classroom. In the doorway stood Mandy, a mischievous smile playing on her lips.

The professor looked up, an annoyed crease appearing on his forehead, but it disappeared as soon as he saw her. She whispered something in his ear, her words too soft for me to hear from where I was sitting.

The room was filled with murmurs from the other students amongst themselves about who she was and how pretty she looked.

"Jim," the professor's voice sliced through the tension in the room, "you're excused from my class today. It's okay, go ahead and good luck."

The words hung heavy in the air, like a verdict being passed. My heart hammered in my chest, a cold fear prickling my skin.

My classmates erupted in cheers, nudging me and egging me on. A flush of embarrassment spread across my cheeks, the heat burning my ears. I hurriedly packed my things, my mind a whirl of confusion and fear. The taste of metal tinged my tongue, a knot forming in my stomach.

Mandy was waiting for me in the hallway, her back against the cold, rough wall. Her uniform seemed even more vibrant under the harsh lights of the corridor. The echo of my classmates' cheers still hung heavy in my ears.

I approached her cautiously, my mind racing with questions.

"What did you tell him?" My voice came out rougher than I had intended. She just smirked, her gaze filled with mischief.

"I told him I was pregnant and that we have an appointment with the OB-GYN." Her words hit me like a punch to the gut. I stared at her, my mind going blank. The faint buzzing of the lights, the distant chatter from the classroom, everything seemed to fade away.

"What the fuck? That's not true!" I protested, my voice rising in panic. The taste of fear was sharp in my mouth, like biting into a lemon. The hallway seemed to spin around me, my vision blurring.

Before I could comprehend what was happening, she grabbed my hand, her grip firm and insistent. She pulled me away from the classroom, leading me out of the campus.

My mind was a whirl of confusion, the world outside felt unreal. I could hear the faint chirping of birds, the rustle of leaves, but it all felt distant, as if I was underwater.

She dragged me out onto the street, the sun beating down on us. The noise of the city rushed back to me, cars honking, people talking, the faint hum of life. I felt a cold sweat trickling down my spine, my heart pounding in my chest.

She pulled me along the crowded streets, weaving us through the bustling city. I didn't know where we were going, but at that moment, I didn't care.

I was lost in a whirlwind of emotions, fear and confusion giving way to a sense of adventure.

We wound up on a bus, the smell of old vinyl and something else that was faintly citrusy filling my nostrils. I was conscious of the rhythmic thrumming of the engine and the soft whirring of the air conditioner.

Mandy was sitting in the seat across the aisle from me, her head propped up against the window, lost in thought.

The afternoon sun bathed the inside of the bus in a warm, orange glow, throwing long shadows across the linoleum floor. I watched as her hair danced in the gentle breeze from the open window. Her silence was unusual, and in that quiet, I could hear the low hum of conversation from the other passengers, the rustle of a newspaper, and the occasional beep of a horn from outside.

Our journey ended at the base of the Statue of Liberty. I stared up at the towering figure in awe, even though I'd seen it countless times before.

She was looking up too, her eyes reflecting the gleaming figure of Lady Liberty. The salty tang of the sea was potent in the air and I could hear the distant cry of seagulls over the muted sounds of the city behind us.

Suddenly, she handed me her phone.

"Take my picture," she demanded, already posing with the statue in the background. I looked at her quizzically, "You're from New York, why are you acting like a tourist?"

She rolled her eyes, "Just take the goddamn picture."

I snapped a few photos, her silhouette framed against the bright afternoon sky. She was radiant, the sunlight creating a halo around her. The click of the camera seemed overly loud in the relative quiet.

After a moment, she gestured for me to join her. I hesitated, "I don't need this. This is dumb," I protested, but she was insistent.

"Just pose and smile."

With an exaggerated sigh, I complied. She pulled me close, her arm snaking around my waist, her phone held up for a selfie. In the frame, our smiles looked almost genuine, a couple of tourists enjoying a beautiful day out.

Soon after, we ended up sitting by the water, the waves lapping gently against the shore. The city's sounds were muted here, replaced by the rhythmic pulse of the sea. The scent of the ocean filled my nostrils, mingling with the faint, earthy aroma of seaweed. The wind carried a chill despite the warmth of the sun overhead.

Tears welled up in her eyes, her gaze fixed on

the horizon. I felt a pang in my chest, a heaviness I didn't know what to do with.

"I wish I could turn back time... or know how to time travel," she said, her voice barely a whisper over the sound of the sea. I frowned, "Why

"Because I don't find any good reason to wake up anymore."

Suddenly, she was pulling off her earrings, chunky little hoops with tiny faux diamonds. Without a word, she threw them into the water.

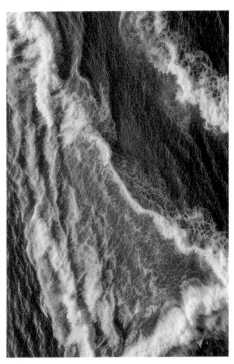

We watched as they glinted in the sunlight before sinking beneath the surface.

"Wow, it's deep," she murmured, her gaze lingering on the spot where her earrings had disappeared.

Her next words were so unexpected they took me by surprise.

"Can you get them for me?" She asked, as if it was the most natural thing in the world. I stared at her, incredulous, "Are you nuts?" I managed to splutter out. But before I could react, she gave me a playful shove towards the water.

For a moment, my heart stopped. The world seemed to slow down. I could see the gleam in her eyes, the wicked smile on her lips. But just as I was about to fall, her hand tightened around my arm, pulling me back.

Her laughter was like a bell, clear and infectious. I couldn't help but join in, my laughter mingling with hers, echoing off the water.

As the laughter died down, I found myself staring at her. The afternoon sun painted her in a soft, golden light, her eyes sparkling with mirth. At that moment, she was more alive than I'd ever seen her.

Chapter 7

∞∞∞

A WEEK HAD PASSED since that strange day at the Statue of Liberty and, somehow, Mandy and I found ourselves wrapped up in this strange dance.

We weren't officially dating and yet, we were seeing each other every day, stealing glances and sharing smiles. There was a peculiar sweetness about this time, a bitter-sweet anticipation that hung between us, but we hadn't yet kissed.

One day, we were sauntering along the bustling streets of New York City, dollar-slice pizzas in hand, the city's cacophony providing a dynamic soundtrack to our aimless amble. The taste of the cheese and tomato sauce on my tongue was potent, the sharp bite of the onions underlain by a sweet tanginess.

She suddenly veered off the sidewalk and perched herself on the steps of a nearby apartment building. She pulled off her high-heeled shoes with a sigh of relief, stretching out her legs in front of her.

I watched as she wriggled her toes, her face screwing up in a grimace before it melted into a look of satisfaction.

"My feet are so tired," she complained, rubbing her soles. She then looked up at me with a glint in her eyes, her fingers tracing the contours of my sneakers.

"Let's trade shoes," she suggested, her tone hopeful. I looked at her then at my own comfortable footwear.

"Not in a million years," I retorted, the thought of squeezing into her heels nothing short of horrifying.

Her lower lip protruded in an exaggerated pout, her eyes shimmering with an unspoken plea.

"Please, pretty please," she coaxed, her fingers now running up my leg. I could feel the softness of her touch, the heat seeping through my jeans.

"I'd rather carry you on my back," I offered, hoping to put an end to this absurd suggestion. Her answer was immediate.

"Nevermind!" she huffed, pulling her hand away.

However, the image of her in distress won me over and, with a sigh of defeat, I unlaced my shoes and handed them to her. The cool pavement felt strange under my sock-clad feet, tiny pebbles digging into my soles.

Her delight at wearing my sneakers was palpable. She wriggled her toes inside them, a sigh of contentment slipping past her lips.

"Wow, this is so comfortable," she announced with a triumphant smile on her face.

In contrast, I was struggling. Her heels were a monstrous invention of mankind. I could feel my toes crunched up against the narrow tip, the straps biting into my skin. The balance was all wrong, and I found myself teetering precariously.

The chuckles from Mandy didn't help either. Yet, there was something undeniably fun about this entire ordeal. The absurdity of it all, the shared laughter—it was moments like these that brought us closer.

Our destination was Central Park, a good three blocks away. It felt like a marathon as I wobbled my way along the sidewalk, Mandy's laughter ringing in my ears.

The soles of my feet were starting to ache, each step more uncomfortable than the last. Yet, the look of joy on her face, the sound of her laughter, made it all worthwhile.

Every step was a trial and every block an achievement. I could feel my calf muscles straining, the pavement rough under my feet. Despite the aching feeling, I realized that I wouldn't trade these moments for anything. This was our dance—unusual, a little painful, but filled with a joy that made every step worth it.

The way Mandy's joy permeated the air was intoxicating. Her laughter was infectious, spreading quickly and infecting even the most stoic of passerby. And then, out of nowhere, she broke into a cartwheel.

Her body twisted in the air with a graceful ease that left me stunned. The world seemed to blur around her as she spun, her hair flying out around her like a halo. I could almost hear the rhythm of her movements, like a silent song that only she could dance to.

"When I was young, I wanted to be a gymnast," she confessed, brushing off her palms and looking up at me with a touch of nostalgia in her eyes.

I took in the way her chest heaved slightly from the exertion, her smile beaming and infectious. I could smell the slight tinge of sweat on her, the scent somehow both sweet and musky. The revelation somehow made sense. Mandy, after all, was a creature of perpetual motion.

Suddenly, her demeanor changed, the effervescence receding as she sat down on a nearby bench, her gaze focused on something distant. Her voice was quiet, almost a whisper against the hum of the city, "Tomorrow is my birthday." Her fingers traced an invisible pattern on the wooden slats of the bench.

Before I could wish her, she added, "I would love to receive a rose. No one has ever given me flowers." Her voice was almost lost in the din of the city, but the undercurrent of melancholy was unmistakable.

I looked at her, really looked at her, and I was baffled.

Mandy was a symphony of beauty and vivaciousness.

"What? That's impossible. You're so pretty," I found myself saying. The words were out before I had a chance to filter them, my own surprise echoing in the space between us.

There was a hint of vulnerability in her eyes as she shot me a small smile, a stark contrast to her usual bravado.

"If you mean it, you will give me flowers during my piano recital tomorrow," she challenged, her voice regaining some of its usual sparkle.

I raised an eyebrow at her, "It's an all-girls school. I won't even be able to get in," I protested.

Her lips curled into a pout as she shrugged nonchalantly, her eyes meeting mine, "It's okay. Don't go then." I could sense the disappointment underlying her attempt at indifference.

Her words hung in the air between us, a silent dare. And I was a sucker for challenges, especially ones posed by Mandy.

As I walked away from her that day, her words echoed in my mind. The sounds of the city faded into the background as I started formulating a plan. I had no idea how I was going to pull it off, but one thing was for sure—I was not going to let Mandy's birthday pass by without a rose from me.

The next day, my heart was in my throat as I stepped off the bus, the bustling cityscape seeming to fade into a distant blur as I approached the imposing iron gates of Mandy's school. My nerves were frayed, my palms sweaty against the cool metal handle of the toolbox I was carrying.

The security guard stationed at the entrance gave me a suspicious once-over, his gaze lingering on my plumber's uniform. It was an old one of my father's, worn and faded with time, but it served the purpose of my disguise.

"I'm here to fix the faculty's pipes," I found myself saying, my voice surprisingly steady despite the thudding in my chest.

The guard eyed me skeptically but nodded and waved me through, the gates creaking open to reveal the vast, manicured grounds beyond. The crisp scent of freshly cut grass filled the air, carrying on it the faint strains of a piano melody that made my heart leap in my chest.

I followed the sound of the music, my steps leading me towards the majestic auditorium. My heart pounded like a wild drum in my chest, each beat echoing with anticipation. The air was thick with the scent of wood and polish, the auditorium boasting an old-world charm that was simultaneously imposing and inviting.

As I stepped inside, the soft, haunting melody of 'Once Upon a December' filled the vast expanse, sending shivers down my spine. And there she was, in the spotlight, her fingers dancing gracefully over the piano keys, her entire being radiating a sort of serene beauty I had never seen before.

Mandy, my Mandy, looked angelic as her body swayed slightly to the rhythm of the music, lost in her own world. The glow from the stage lights illuminated her face, casting her in an ethereal light that took my breath away. My heart throbbed in my chest as I stood there, spellbound by the mesmerizing sight before me.

Taking a deep breath to steady my nerves, I began my approach, the toolbox heavy in my hands. The echo of my footsteps felt thunderous in the silence, but she seemed oblivious, completely absorbed in her music. The soft notes of the piano filled the room, wrapping around us like a warm blanket.

As the music ebbed and the final note resonated in the air, I found myself on the stage. My hands felt cold against the warm metal of the toolbox, the anticipation gnawing at my insides. I opened the box, revealing the single red rose nestled within, its scent a stark contrast to the sharp tang of metal and grease.

The auditorium erupted into cheers and applause as I handed her the rose, my heart hammering against my ribcage. She looked at me, her eyes wide in surprise, the rose held delicately in her hands.

"Happy birthday, Mandy."

Time seemed to slow as she leaned in, and before I knew what was happening, her lips were on mine.

The world fell away in that moment, everything else blurring into insignificance. The taste of her lips, sweet and warm, was intoxicating. Her perfume, a soft blend of vanilla and roses, filled my senses, making my head spin. The cheers and applause from the audience sounded like a distant echo, drowned out by the pounding in my ears.

Her lips moved against mine with a surprising gentleness, sending sparks of heat coursing through my veins. I was vaguely aware of my hand reaching up to cradle her face, the silky strands of her hair slipping through my fingers. Her skin felt warm under my touch, a stark contrast to the cold metal of the toolbox still clutched in my other hand.

I don't know how long we stood there, locked in our first kiss, but it felt both like an eternity and a fleeting moment. The world had narrowed down to Mandy and me, our lips moving in a slow, sweet dance. The smell of her, the taste of her, the feel of her—everything was imprinted into my senses, a memory I would cherish forever.

Two weeks had passed since that unforgettable day at Mandy's school when my phone buzzed with a sudden urgency. "Emergency... Mt. Sinai... Critical condition... Mandy," the disjointed text messages said from an unfamiliar number left my heart pounding in my chest.

The blare of sirens and the frenetic energy of the city seemed distant as I dashed for the bus. A cold fear twisted in my gut, my palms clammy and my breath coming in ragged gasps. Every beat of my heart echoed with Mandy's name, each pulse a silent plea to whatever powers that be.

The bus ride felt like a lifetime, each red light a piercing stab of delay. As I disembarked and rushed into the hospital's sterile halls, the sharp smell of disinfectant and sickness filled my nostrils. My heart hammered a staccato rhythm against my ribs, my breath shaky as I approached the reception desk, Mandy's name stumbling from my lips.

The nurse pointed me towards a room, her voice a soothing balm to my spiraling thoughts. As I ran down the hallway, my senses were assaulted by the harsh fluorescent lights, the steady beep of monitors, the muted whispers of staff and patients. The stark white walls felt cold and unwelcoming, my footfalls echoing ominously.

I found her with her foot bandaged up, propped on a pillow, and looking decidedly not on death's door. My heart did a somersault of relief, then immediately twisted in a knot of annoyance.

"What happened?" I blurted out, my relief doing little to quell my anger.

She looked up, and to my surprise, she started laughing. Her eyes sparkled with mischief as she said, "I sprained my ankle." I stared at her, my mind reeling.

This was the emergency?

This was her critical condition?

I felt like a balloon that had been deflated, my worry seeping out of me and replaced with exasperation.

"I skipped my class because you said it was an emergency and you were in critical condition," I retorted, irritation edging my words.

But she only laughed more, declaring her sprained ankle to be 'really critical.'

As my confusion grew, she produced a second phone from her bag, her grin growing even wider as she revealed that she had sent the messages herself. I could only gape at her, flabbergasted. She explained that she had twisted her ankle during volleyball practice, her tone casual as if she hadn't just scared the living daylights out of me.

Feeling both relieved and exasperated, I sank into the chair beside her bed, the chill of the metal frame seeping through my clothes. The hospital room was a stark contrast to the vibrant world outside, its sterile environment filled with a sense of unease.

She looked at me, her mirth subsiding as she noted my agitation. She then reached out, her hand warm against my forearm as she asked me to sit with her. Despite my annoyance, I found myself softening under her touch, my anger melting away under her earnest gaze.

I sighed, rubbing a hand over my face as I asked, "How long until it heals?"

Her smile faltered slightly as she revealed the doctor's prognosis—a month. My heart sank at the news, my annoyance with her antics fading as I realized the gravity of her situation.

As I sat there, holding her hand in the cold, sterile hospital room, the gravity of the situation hit me. Mandy, my vibrant, spontaneous Mandy, was sidelined for a month. And despite the initial scare, I found myself thankful that it was just a sprain.

She cleared her throat, interrupting the silence that had fallen between us. The sudden seriousness of her expression had me sitting up straighter, my annoyance with her earlier antics quickly fading. Her voice was low, just above a whisper when she confessed, "There's something else, Jim."

Her words hung heavy in the air between us, a quiet desperation in her eyes. She confessed about a charity ball she was supposed to attend in a week, one where she was to be one of the models. The proceeds of the event were to go towards a noble cause, to help orphaned children from parents who had suffered from drug and alcohol abuse.

My stomach dropped as I listened, the real weight of her situation sinking in. Mandy, despite her eccentricities, was deeply committed to causes like this. Her heart bled for others in a way that humbled me. It was one of the things I admired most about her.

"But what does this have to do with your ankle?" I asked, already fearing the answer. Her ankle would still be healing by then, making it impossible for her to walk in the show.

The loss of one model might not seem like a big deal, but the dress she was supposed to wear was one of the most expensive pieces. Its sale alone could raise a significant amount for the cause.

She paused, her eyes searching mine. Then she hit me with it.

"I need you to do it for me."

I blinked, certain I hadn't heard her correctly.

"What? Mandy, I can't wear a dress. I'm a guy!"

"But everyone can wear a dress," she retorted, an earnest pleading in her eyes.

"Think about those poor children. This is their chance at a better life. We can't let my sprained ankle get in the way. I'd rather give the model's talent fee to the children."

Her words hung in the air between us, her plea sending a jolt of guilt through me. I felt like I was teetering on the edge of a cliff, about to make a decision that would push me into the unknown.

"But it's just for one night," she reasoned, seeing my hesitance. Her hand squeezed mine, her touch grounding me amidst the whirlwind of thoughts. The scent of her perfume, sweet and floral, filled my senses, grounding me to the moment.

She was right. It was only for a night, but it was a night that could change lives, give hope to children who desperately needed it.

But, God, a dress? The very thought sent my nerves into a tailspin.

And yet, I found myself looking into her hopeful eyes, her faith in me unwavering despite my reservations. The hum of the hospital around us faded, replaced by the steady beat of my heart, its rhythm seemingly in sync with the silent plea in her gaze.

Finally, I let out a resigned sigh. I had been brought up to help others when they needed it, and right now, Mandy needed me. Those children needed me. And if it meant wearing a dress for a night, well, it was a small price to pay.

"Alright," I muttered, trying to suppress the blush creeping up my neck.

"I'll do it." Her face lit up, her joy shining brighter than any hospital light. And with that, I found myself reluctantly agreeing to step into Mandy's shoes, quite literally.

Chapter 8

∞∞∞

T HE FIRST TIME I MET MANDY'S FATHER, I was already strung out on nerves. But walking into their grand penthouse suite in Manhattan, all six bedrooms and sprawling living spaces a testament to their opulence, had my head spinning.

She took my hand and led me inside, her presence a soothing balm on my fraying nerves.

"Dad, this is Jim," she introduced, her voice echoing in the vast expanse of the living room. Her father looked up from his paper, a pair of piercing blue eyes settling on me. I swallowed hard, the silence in the room deafening.

"He's my boyfriend," she added, her words igniting a spark of hope within me. I'd been waiting for her to acknowledge what we had for weeks now. The stern man merely nodded in my direction, offering no more than an 'Hmm,' before turning his attention back to his work.

His indifference stung, but Mandy was already pulling me away, leading me towards her room. A tingle of anticipation spread through me as I stepped into her sanctuary. It was every bit as girly as I had imagined, a shrine to her love for music and all things pink.

"Excited?" she asked—referring to the makeover she had planned, her eyes twinkling with mischief. I snorted, shaking my head, "No way."

Her laughter rang out, filling the room with warmth. She reached up to pinch my nose playfully, a mischievous glint in her eyes.

"Well, you should be. Take your clothes off, honey."

My heart thundered in my chest, excitement washing over me from what she just said.

Was this it?

Was this the moment I had been waiting for?

Was she talking about making love?

The air in the room felt charged, my senses heightening as she watched me expectantly.

Just as I was about to start undressing, she burst into the room carrying a pot of hot wax and strips. The smirk on her face said it all.

"Oh wow," she teased, her eyes drifting downwards.

"I didn't know you were that... packed."

My face flushed with heat at her comment, her cheeky touch of my penis doing nothing to help. She giggled at my reaction, batting my hands away when I tried to cover myself.

"We're not here for that, lover boy," she scolded playfully, "We need to make you hairless from head to toe."

My mind reeled at the thought. Waxing? All over?

"I thought I was going to score," I mumbled, her laughter echoing in my ears. My nerves were back with a vengeance, fear prickling at the back of my mind.

Would it hurt?

How bad would it be?

She must've noticed my apprehension, because her expression softened.

"Relax, it won't be that bad," she reassured, her hand finding mine. Her touch grounded me, her scent filling my senses. And with that, we began the process, one that would surely be seared into my memory for a long time to come.

"Face first," she said, brandishing the waxing stick with a glint in her eyes. My breath hitched as I felt the hot wax being applied to my skin. I had never paid much attention to the stubble that graced my face until she decided it had to go.

The scent of the wax filled the air, the thick substance clinging to my skin.

"Ready?" She asked, the devilish grin on her face making my stomach drop.

I took a deep breath and gave a brisk nod. Before I could change my mind, she had ripped off the strip. A sting coursed through my skin.

"Fffuuuckk!" I tried to laugh it off, but the lingering burn was a stark reminder of what was to come. She simply giggled, her fingers softly tracing over the newly smooth skin. The feeling was odd, but not unpleasant, a mixture of sensitivity and tenderness.

Next came the armpits. I'd never given much thought to the hair that sprouted from there, but she had other plans. The feeling of the wax against my skin, a hot slither of discomfort, had me clenching my teeth.

Her hands moved swiftly, smearing on the

wax and pressing the strips onto the hair-laden skin. The tension in the air was palpable, my senses honed in on every touch and sensation. The rip of the strips, the echoes of her laughter, the taste of apprehension on my tongue... it was all-consuming.

Before I could protest, she moved onto the next area. As the wax made contact with my pubic region, I let out a yelp. It was one thing to deal with the occasional pain in my face and armpits, but this was a different level.

"Relax," she soothed, her laughter filling the room.

"We're almost there." The anticipation was killing me. As she ripped off the strip, my body tensed, a profanity slipping past my lips. The stinging sensation was momentary, but intense.

Once the initial shock had passed, I was oddly aware of the smoothness that had replaced the familiar coarseness. It felt weird and incredibly sensitive.

The room was filled with the scent of the wax, the laughter, and my occasional yelps. She seemed to be enjoying herself immensely, her eyes dancing with amusement as she moved onto my legs.

The process repeated, a rhythmic pattern of wax, press, and rip.

Each pull of the strip sent a jolt of pain through me, my nerves screaming in protest. But with each strip, the sensation lessened, replaced by the soft, sensitive skin underneath.

It was a peculiar feeling, the hairlessness oddly freeing. I was acutely aware of everything —the smoothness of my skin, the cool touch of her fingers, the scent of the wax, the taste of anticipation.

It was an assault on my senses, but not in an unpleasant way.

And then, Mandy announced it was time for the last part.

"Is that really necessary?" I stammered, my eyes wide with fear.

She let out a peal of laughter, her amusement evident.

"I have OCD, we have to get everything off," she declared, her voice laced with laughter. I sighed deeply, resigned to my fate. If I had thought the previous waxing was uncomfortable, I was in for a rude awakening.

"Bend over," she said as she guided me on the floor and caressed my butt cheeks for the impending challenge.

I won't get into the details, but let's just say the final process was an experience that left me breathless and swearing. Mandy, on the other hand, seemed to find it amusing, her laughter filling the room as she finished up.

By the time we were done, my body was a canvas of red and tingling skin, the absence of hair a foreign sensation. But as I looked at her, her smile brighter than the stars, I couldn't bring myself to regret it.

After all, it was just one night. What could possibly go wrong?

She then vanished into her walk-in closet, reappearing moments later with an armful of lingerie and what she referred to as 'shapewear.'

"You might be sexy, Jim, but you're not exactly shapely," she stated, her words tumbling out in a rush of laughter. It took a moment for her statement to register in my mind, my eyes widening as I took in the array of undergarments she had procured.

As she began to explain the purpose of each item, I found myself becoming engrossed in the process. I hadn't realized the lengths women went to in order to mold their bodies into societal expectations of beauty.

It was an awakening of sorts, a glimpse into the world Mandy navigated every day. The touch of the fabric against my skin, the chill of the room, the faint whiff of her perfume in the air—every sense was heightened, every emotion magnified.

She began with the shapewear, a snug-fitting garment that promised to pull in my waist and enhance my hips.

"This will give you a more feminine figure," she said, her fingers tracing the lines of my body through the fabric. The feeling of the fabric against my skin was oddly comfortable, a gentle pressure that reshaped my figure.

Next came the lingerie. As she handed me a delicate pair of panties, she glanced at my crotch with a mischievous smile.

"Now comes the tricky part," she giggled. Her hands moved expertly, adjusting my penis as she guided me on how to tuck. The sensation was unlike anything I had ever felt before, a bizarre combination of discomfort and arousal.

"Stop getting hard!" she exclaimed, her cheeks flushing a brilliant shade of red. The scent of her shampoo filled my nostrils, the taste of my own embarrassment lingering on my tongue. My heart pounded in my chest, a rush of adrenaline coursing through my veins.

"I can't help it," I groaned, "you're touching it!" Mandy burst into laughter, the sound filling the room and dispelling the awkwardness.

Her hand brushed against mine, the cool touch a stark contrast to the heat coursing through me. I could hear her laughter ringing in my ears and see the humor twinkling in her eyes. It was a moment of connection, a shared experience that was as strange as it was intimate.

We continued to laugh, the tension in the room dissolving into the air. The room was filled with the sounds of our amusement, the scent of the lingerie, the sight of my body dressed in women's undergarments. It was all so surreal, a moment of pure ridiculousness that somehow managed to feel strangely liberating.

Once we had composed ourselves, she moved on to the next set of garments. With each new piece, I found myself becoming more comfortable in the clothes, the strange sensation of femininity settling around me like a warm blanket.

The next step in my transformation, according to Mandy, was makeup. A smorgasbord of cosmetics was laid out before me, a cacophony of colors and strange tools.

She looked at me, eyes sparkling, as she held the foundation in her hand.

"Alright, Jim, close your eyes. And no peeking!" I complied, feeling the cool slick of the makeup against my skin.

"Feels like you're smearing pudding on my face," I commented. She just laughed, her fingers deftly blending the makeup.

After a few minutes of what felt like face-painting, she picked up a pencil-like thing.

"This is called a kohl pencil. Stay still, don't squint."

Easier said than done. I flinched as she brought it close, my eyes watering.

"You alright?" she asked, grinning. I rolled my eyes, doing my best not to smear the makeup.

"I'm surviving. It's just... you poking my eye is not on my bucket list."

Next came the wig. "You know, this feels kind of like a scalp massage," I commented as she adjusted it on my head. She just snorted, her hands gently tucking in stray hairs.

"No. You're not going to convert this into a spa treatment."

"Wow!" she giggled as she brushed my newfound golden locks, "you're even prettier than me!" My comeback was swift, "Well, girls do call me a pretty boy, you know."

Teaching me how to walk was an exercise in hilarity. Mandy trying to imitate a supermodel while I tried not to stumble was a sight.

"Keep your back straight, chin up. Walk like

you're kissing the ground with your feet, not stomping grapes for wine!" she instructed.

Putting on the dress was a struggle, I felt like a toddler trying to put on his clothes for the first time. She was trying hard not to laugh, her giggles only causing me to fumble more.

And just like that, the evening was over. It was like a bizarre dream, stepping out of my skin and into someone else's. After all, how often does a guy get to walk a mile in a woman's high-heels and a designer dress, all for a good cause?

Chapter 9

∞∞∞

THE NIGHT we've been waiting for has finally arrived. Backstage, the atmosphere was electric. Frenzied makeup artists, chatter of models, and the distant hum of the audience. Amid all of it, Mandy was my rock, standing on her crutch and bandaged foot, a determined look on her face.

"Jim," she began, her tone all business, "remember, one foot in front of the other, shoulders back, and for god's sake, don't look like you've seen a ghost."

A makeup artist rushed over, brushes at the ready. As she leaned in, she raised a hand.

"Go easy on the eye makeup," she instructed, "we don't want him looking like a raccoon." She glanced at me, winking as if we were partners in crime.

The artist raised an eyebrow but nodded, blending in softer shades on my eyelids.

A rush of nerves hit me as the moment came nearer. I was in a dress, in a wig, about to walk down a catwalk for the first time in my life. I could feel the adrenaline pumping, my heartbeat in my ears.

She squeezed my hand, her voice cutting through my anxiety.

"You got this. It's just like our practice. Besides, you look stunning."

The curtains were drawn back. The lights were so bright they practically swallowed the audience, their applause washing over me like a wave. As I took my first step onto the stage, my dress' designer's name *Yves Saint Laurent* was announced and a barrage of camera flashes hit me, blinding and disorienting.

Ignoring the starbursts in my vision, I put one foot in front of the other, remembering her words. The cool air from the auditorium caressed my skin, carrying the faint scent of perfume and excitement.

I focused on the rhythm of my heels against the stage, the low click-clack drowned out by the music and the applause. The paparazzi at the front

LILLY LUSTWOOD

were shouting, "Bella Ciao, what's your name?"

As the lights refracted off their lenses, I turned to them, giving them my best mysterious smile, playing the part of the enigmatic model.

The crowd erupted, cheering and clapping as I twirled at the end of the runway. I could hear Mandy's distinctive cheer from backstage, her voice as warm and encouraging as always. A wash of relief and joy flooded over me.

I was doing it, I was really doing it.

Stepping back from the edge, I began to make my way back, my heart pounding in my chest. I could feel the silk of the dress swaying with my movements, the hair of the wig tickling my shoulders.

As I took my final steps and disappeared behind the curtain, the audience's applause was still ringing in my ears.

After the show, we found ourselves in a room both familiar to us. The room was a budget motel standard, tacky wallpaper and a queen-size bed covered with a faded, floral bedspread. Mandy was perched on the edge, her crutches leaning against the wall. She'd popped open a bottle of cheap wine, pouring the burgundy liquid into plastic motel cups.

We were celebrating, just the two of us. Too shy to hit the clubs while I was still in the dress, we'd decided to keep the party private. We clinked cups, her eyes sparkling with mischief.

"To the most stunning model on the stage tonight," she toasted.

The wine went down with a warm burn, loosening my nerves and letting the reality of the day wash over me. Laughter bubbled up from me, a feeling of lightness taking over.

"I can't believe I just did that," I confessed, reaching for my glass again.

She put her cup down, her eyes lingering on mine.

"I can," she said softly. Her hand reached out, fingers tracing up my leg, over the sheer stocking. It sent shivers up my spine, the lightest touch feeling amplified on my skin.

She leaned in, her lips capturing mine in a kiss that felt different. Intense. It wasn't the playful pecks from before, this was passionate, full of longing. She pulled back slightly, her breath hitching.

"You're so sexy, Jimmy baby, my pretty boy."

Her words hit me like a jolt, sending heat

coursing through me. Our lips met again, more urgently this time. My hand found its way to her breast, cupping it through her blouse. Her soft moan filled the room, her fingers tugging at the blonde wig on my head.

The pain from the tucked-away arousal was growing unbearable, but it was drowned out by the intoxicating thrill of the moment.

I was about to slip my hand under her skirt, heart pounding with anticipation when she suddenly pulled away. Her breathing was ragged, her eyes wide.

"I'm sorry," she stammered out, her voice barely a whisper, "I can't do this."

Before I could process her words, she had grabbed her crutch and was hobbling towards the door. My mind was racing, trying to make sense of what had just happened. The door clicked shut behind her, leaving me alone in the motel room.

I was left high and dry, the intimacy of the moment vanished, replaced with a creeping emptiness. The faint scent of her perfume hung in the air, a cruel reminder of what had just been ripped away.

I sat there in stunned silence, my mind still reeling, heart pounding with confusion and frustration. The night that had started with such promise ended with an unexpected and sudden jolt.

The quiet of the motel room was deafening. I was alone, still in the borrowed finery, still wearing Mandy's perfume. Questions spun around in my mind like dervishes.

Why had she left?

What had gone wrong?

It was like standing at the edge of a cliff, the solid ground of understanding crumbling away beneath me.

I looked down at myself, at the shapewear hugging my form, the dress that clung to the curves I never knew I had. Could it be the clothes?

The feminine facade I wore for the night?

Yet, she'd said I was sexy. Her voice echoed in my head, the way her eyes had sparkled when she said it. She hadn't recoiled from me; she'd leaned in, drawn to me. The clothes couldn't be it.

Was it because she was saving herself? A

pledge to celibacy until marriage, a promise she wasn't ready to break. I thought back to all the times we'd hung out, all the clues she might have dropped, intentionally or not.

But I couldn't recall a single instance where she had hinted at such a conviction.

She'd been open about so much, why not this?

My heart pounded in my chest, the silence of the room amplifying the beat. I ran my fingers over the lace trim of the dress, the soft fabric a stark contrast to the turmoil inside me.

My skin was still sensitive from the waxing, every touch a stark reminder of the lengths I had gone to for her, for this night.

Could it be that she was a virgin?

Was that why she ran?

The idea made sense but it also didn't. Mandy was beautiful, she was confident and she was loved by many. The idea that she'd never been with someone else before was hard to swallow.

But then again, we all have our secrets, right? Maybe this was hers.

In the glow of the single bedside lamp,

my shadow loomed large and distorted on the wall. It was as if the room itself was taunting me, stretching the confusion and doubts into monstrous proportions.

I felt a cold chill despite the heavy New York summer heat seeping in through the half-open window.

I let my fingers trace over my shaven legs, the smooth sensation alien and yet familiar. A shiver ran up my spine. I felt vulnerable, stripped bare both emotionally and physically, in a way I hadn't before.

The faint hum of traffic outside was the only sound accompanying my thoughts. I strained my ears, half-hoping, half-dreading to hear her voice, her footsteps, but there was nothing. The night pressed in, heavy with unspoken words and a narrative that seemed to have veered off course.

The lingering scent of her perfume seemed to grow stronger, filling my nostrils and making my head spin. I closed my eyes, trying to shut out the room, the dress, the smell. But even behind closed eyelids, her face was all I could see.

Chapter 10

∞∞∞

THE MORNING SUN WAS ALREADY HIGH when I got the text. Mandy wanted to meet at the park, by the largest fig tree on campus. A flutter of hope stirred within me, but it was mired in a sea of unanswered questions. My mind was a whirlwind, thoughts spinning too fast to catch.

With a heart that pounded like a drum, I made my way to the park. The air was warm, the scent of summer and freshly mowed grass filling my nostrils. Birds sang in the trees, their songs a sweet symphony against the backdrop of my internal turmoil.

There she was, sitting under the massive fig tree, her silhouette framed by the leafy green canopy. Her figure was smaller from afar, delicate against the vast backdrop of the park. I wanted to run to her, to ask her a thousand questions, to hold her close. But something held me back, a fear of what she might say, of what her answers might be.

She held out an envelope, her hands trembling. There was a wetness in her eyes, the first sign of tears.

"I wrote a letter," she said, her voice barely more than a whisper.

"Read it after a year, same time, same date, same place." Her words hung in the air between us, a promise and a puzzle all at once.

Then she dropped another bombshell. She was leaving, going to study in Brazil. She already had the tickets. My heart clenched in my chest, a fist squeezing the life out of it. Brazil. A country, a culture, a life so far from our shared reality, it was hard to comprehend.

From her pocket, she pulled out a pair of gloves and a lunch box.

She put the letter inside the box, a sacred ritual of sorts. She was serious about this. As serious as I've ever seen her.

"You can't read it," she warned, tears streaming down her face.

"If you do, I won't show up again."

It was too much. The park, the summer air,

the fig tree—everything blurred as tears welled up in my own eyes. I knelt down and started digging, my hands shaking. The soft earth gave way under my hands, the cool dirt a stark contrast against my burning skin.

"Please," I begged, the words choked out between sobs.

"Why are you leaving? Was all this just a game to you?" My heart ached, the pain a physical force that threatened to tear me apart.

She just shook her head, silent tears streaming down her face.

"No, you'll understand in a year," she whispered, her voice barely audible.

"Thank you for everything, Jim." Those were her final words, a farewell that rang hollow in the face of my desperation.

Suddenly, two men appeared. They pushed me away, breaking the connection. I was left staring at her retreating figure, my heart screaming in protest. Then, she was gone. Swallowed by the crowd, lost among the faces of strangers.

I was left alone under the tree, my heartache a

solitary symphony echoing through the park.

"Why?" I whispered to the empty air, my words lost in the gentle rustle of the leaves. I was alone again, left with nothing but the promise of a letter, a year from now.

The rest of the day was a blur. I couldn't concentrate, couldn't think, couldn't breathe. I felt numb, a hollow shell of a person. The world moved around me, life continued in its usual pace, but I was stuck.

Stuck in the pain, in the confusion, in the why.

The sun set, casting long shadows that stretched out towards me, as if trying to pull me into the darkness. I sat under the fig tree once more, the envelope buried under the earth a cruel reminder of the day's events.

I was alone. Alone with my questions, my heartache, my confusion.

I felt hollow, a shell of the person I used to be. She had left, leaving behind a promise, a riddle, and a heartache that seemed to consume me.

As night fell, I stayed under the fig tree, my heart as heavy as the silence around me. Her absence was a gaping wound, raw and aching. And in the quiet of the night, I could only wonder, why?

Why had she left?

Why couldn't she stay?

But the night offered no answers. Only silence, and the distant echo of my own heartbreak. I was alone, lost in a sea of unanswered questions, clinging onto a promise made under a fig tree. And all I could do was wait. Wait for a year, for a letter, for answers that might never come.

It was almost a year since Mandy had left me, a year of questions, doubts, and a gnawing emptiness. Life had gone on, despite the hole in my heart.

School was demanding, final semester and all that. My buddies Vinny and Marco were as engrossed in their projects as I was in mine. We were required to create a pitch deck, and the goal was to secure actual investors.

The hustle was real, and yet, in the midst of all this, I couldn't forget about Mandy.

An alarm blared from my phone, shattering my concentration. The screen blinked, displaying today's date and time. A pang of realization hit me.

It was the day, the exact moment a year ago when Mandy had handed me the letter under the fig tree.

A lump formed in my throat as I made my way to the park. The scent of fresh green leaves and the earthy musk of the fig tree sent a shiver down my spine. My heart pounded in my chest as I neared the massive tree. I took a deep breath, knelt down and began to dig.

I unearthed the lunch box, now caked with a year's worth of dirt. Inside, the envelope looked as pristine as the day she had sealed it. I pulled it out and opened it with trembling hands.

Mandy's handwriting was beautiful, every stroke of the pen filled with a grace that was quintessentially her. As I began to read, her voice echoed in my head, as clear as if she was standing right there with me.

She confessed in the letter that she was a transgender woman. She had been terrified that I'd leave if I found out. The words stung. It wasn't her being a transgender woman that hurt, it was the fact that she didn't trust me enough to tell me.

That she felt she had to hide her truth from me.

She wasn't in Brazil. She was in an alcoholics anonymous program, dealing with the loss of a man who had loved her for who she was. A man, she said, I reminded her of. The pain in her words was palpable, etched deep within every line of the letter.

Then came the revelation that shattered my heart anew. She had been planning to end her life when I saved her. The woman I loved had been so deeply in pain, so utterly lost, and I had been oblivious.

The letter ended with a confession of love and a plea for forgiveness. She hoped that if we were meant to be, we would find each other again.

Tears blurred my vision, each word of her letter echoing in my mind. I crumpled the letter in my hands, my heart heavy with a multitude of emotions.

"I don't care if you're a transgender woman," I whispered to the wind.

"I love you."

I waited under the fig tree for what seemed like an eternity, the sun beginning to set, casting long shadows. But she didn't show up. A dull ache settled in my chest, my mind filled with thoughts of what could have been.

After three long hours, Vinny and Marco found me. Their faces were etched with concern. They pulled me to my feet, their arms around my shoulders.

"Let's just drink, bro," they said, their voices filled with understanding.

So we left the park, the fig tree, and Mandy's letter behind. I couldn't help but look back one last time. I had come looking for answers, for closure. But all I found were more questions and a deeper longing for a woman who was lost to me.

In my heart, I knew Mandy was not just a memory. She was a part of me, a part that I would carry with me, always. And though she wasn't physically with me, in my heart, she never left.

Chapter 11

∞∞∞

THE NEXT MORNING, my mom busied herself with fixing my tie. "Oh, I don't know what to do with you," she lamented, her brow furrowing in exasperation.

"You're going to be a businessman but can't even fix your own tie."

I could smell her perfume, a delicate blend of roses and vanilla that reminded me of my childhood. The sight of her hands, so nimble and delicate, working on my tie, brought a strange sense of comfort. It felt like a mother's love woven into a simple act of care.

My dad stood by the doorway, his arms crossed over his chest and a proud smile playing on his lips.

"I'm so proud of you, son," he declared, his deep voice resonating through the room. I could feel the sincerity behind his words. It warmed me, fueling my confidence. His eyes shone with a mix of pride and anticipation.

"Now, Mrs. Wortham is very rich," my mom continued as she finished with my tie, her hands smoothing down my shirt.

"And we're so lucky that she somehow remembers me from college. We can't embarrass ourselves. You're so lucky she agreed to be part of your project."

As she chattered on, I could sense the nervous energy radiating from her. It was contagious. My heart pounded a bit harder, my palms grew slightly clammy. A lump of anxiety formed in my throat.

Before we knew it, we were on our way to The Plaza Hotel's restaurant. We rode in a limousine borrowed from my father's friend. The limo was plush and lavish, with the scent of expensive leather and faint cologne permeating the interior.

I could hear the hum of the city outside, muffled by the thick glass windows. We moved through the bustling traffic of Manhattan, the city's skyscrapers towering above us. The air inside the limo was heavy with tension, anticipation for the meeting bubbling beneath the surface.

My mom kept primping me, straightening my

tie, smoothing down my hair.

"Remember your manners, Jim Forrest," she reminded me for the umpteenth time. My dad chuckled, his hearty laugh breaking the tension in the limo.

The Plaza Hotel came into view, its grand architecture a testament to the city's rich history. My heart pounded in my chest. Mrs. Wortham was waiting, and the future of our project hinged on this meeting.

As we stepped out of the limo, the cool Manhattan air hit us. It was a beautiful day, the sun casting long shadows across the cityscape. The smell of the city, a mixture of the nearby Central Park and the tantalizing aroma of street food, filled my nostrils.

The hustle and bustle of the city faded as we entered the hotel, replaced by the soft murmurs of patrons and the clinking of silverware.

The restaurant inside was even more stunning than I'd imagined. Crystal chandeliers hung from the high ceilings, casting a soft light over the beautifully arranged tables. The rich aroma of gourmet food filled the air, making my stomach growl in anticipation.

As we were led to our table, my parents by my side, I couldn't help but feel a surge of pride. I had made it this far. I was about to pitch my project to one of the wealthiest women in the city.

My heart raced with a mix of anticipation, excitement, and a healthy dose of fear. But amidst all the emotions swirling inside me, I knew one thing for certain—I was ready.

Seeing Mrs. Wortham in person was intimidating. She held herself with a grace and authority that commanded respect. But as soon as she laid eyes on my mom, her eyes lit up with an infectious enthusiasm, transforming her stern demeanor into one of warm familiarity.

They both were giddy with excitement as they reminisced about their college days. I listened as they exchanged tales of their youth, their laughter blending with the background music in the restaurant.

The air was filled with the sound of their laughter, and the room smelled like nostalgia, with a hint of the rich food being served around us. The taste of the appetizers seemed to fade into the background as their stories took center stage.

At first, their exchange was nerve-wracking. Every chuckle and gasp made my heart skip a beat. But as they delved deeper into their past, the tension melted away.

They were not a successful businesswoman and a struggling mother anymore—they were two old friends catching up after a long time. Their chatter became a comforting hum in the background.

Suddenly, a familiar face walked in and sat beside Mrs. Wortham. I froze. It was Mandy. Her hair was shorter now, and she carried herself with a confidence I hadn't seen before. But her eyes were the same—the same bright, expressive eyes that had captivated me.

She seemed equally surprised to see me. For a moment, we just stared at each other, a whirlpool of emotions swirling between us. The noise around us seemed to fade away, replaced by the loud thumping of my heart in my ears. The world narrowed down to just the two of us.

Mrs. Wortham's voice broke the silence.

"This is my daughter, Mandy," she introduced,

her eyes twinkling with pride.

My parents were visibly taken aback, but they quickly composed themselves.

"She's so beautiful, just like you," my mom

cooed, her eyes gleaming with admiration.

All the while, Mandy and I remained locked in a silent conversation. There were so many things we wanted to say, so many feelings we wanted to express. But all that came out was a choked whisper from my lips.

"I still love you," I mouthed, tears brimming in my eyes.

Her eyes widened slightly, a single tear rolling down her cheek. I wished I could reach out to her, to tell her that I meant every word. But all I could do was sit there, my heart pounding in my chest, the taste of regret bitter on my tongue. The rich aroma of food, the soft music, the clinking of glasses, everything seemed to fade away. All that mattered was Mandy and the love that still lingered between us.

She blinked, her lashes damp with unshed tears, her lips trembling as she held my gaze. There was a silent understanding between us, a shared history that was etched into the very essence of our beings. For that fleeting moment, it felt like we were the only two people in the room.

As I looked at her one last time, I knew that

this was not the end of our journey. It was just another chapter in our tangled, messy, beautiful love story.

Epilogue

∞ ∞ ∞

THE MORNING SUN PEEKED through the small gaps in the bedroom blinds, warming my face and waking me from a restful slumber. I groaned, but not out of irritation. It was a groan of contentment, of pure, unadulterated happiness.

Beside me, Mandy stirred, her long lashes fluttering open to reveal those bright hazel eyes that still mesmerized me every day. Her bare shoulder glowed under the soft morning light, the sheets pooling around her waist.

She was beautiful. No, more than that. She was ethereal.

A year had passed since that fateful dinner at The Plaza. A year since our lives became inexplicably entwined once again. I was no longer just a university student grappling with my emotions, struggling to come to terms with Mandy's departure.

I was a graduate, working in Mrs. Wortham's marketing firm alongside Mandy. We were a team in every sense of the word.

As I watched her stretch and yawn, her lips curving into a sleepy smile, I traced the familiar contours of her face. Her skin was soft against my fingers, the subtle hint of her floral perfume filling my senses. My heart swelled with love.

"I love you, Jim," she murmured, reaching over to lace her fingers with mine. Her admission was met with a broad smile, my response echoing in the quiet room.

"I love you too, Mandy."

A year on, our relationship had grown stronger. Her past wasn't a shadow lurking behind us anymore. It was a part of her, a part that made her the woman I loved. Her strength, her courage, and her resilience were inspiring.

Work was a different ballgame altogether. Working with her had its perks—stolen kisses in the elevator, secret lunch dates in the nearby café, and impromptu brainstorming sessions that often ended up with us sprawled on the floor amidst a sea of blueprints and designs.

It wasn't always rainbows and sunshine, of course. There were disagreements, intense debates, and the occasional heated argument. But in the end, we always found a way to reconcile our differences and move forward.

The past year had been a whirlwind of emotions, but every moment had been worth it. From standing on the stage in front of investors, nervously pitching our ideas, to late-night brainstorming sessions in our shared apartment, we had built something meaningful.

Life had a funny way of throwing curveballs at you. When I'd first met Mandy, I'd never imagined the journey we'd embark on together. It was a journey that taught me about love, acceptance, and the importance of staying true to oneself. And I wouldn't trade my crazy girl with anyone in this world.

THE END <3

Did you enjoy My Crazy Girl? In that case, I hope you could check out my bundle Feminization Fantasies.

It contains five of my chart-topping illustrated feminization and transgender transformation steamy romances.

Story 1 – Girthy Girl

I've never lost a case and I topped the bar exams. Discipline came naturally but why was it so hard to resist the tactile feeling of silk and stockings brushing against my hairless legs?

Story 2 – The Doctor is In

He was the best cosmetic surgeon in the city and my career as a new nurse highly depended on his recommendation. In too deep, I allowed him to fill me in the most intimate places and completely change my wardrobe.

Story 3 – Island Princess

It wasn't exactly a lovely day to go scuba diving, but it was the perfect day to be washed away and be rescued and feminized by a hunky prince.

Story 4 – Red Light Sissy

I had to know her. I had to get her story. But I didn't have the money to do so. The free way to do it was to dress up like her, I thought.

Little did I know, it entailed more than standing on the street corner in a long brown wig, a tight red dress, chewing gum, and marching in fishnet stockings and high-heeled boots.

Story 5 – Royally Switched

When my sister badgered me into going to Paris, I was fine with carrying her bags and pretending to enjoy the sights and sounds of the city.

Little did I know, the trip that she had planned all her life would drastically change mine, with a bonus of chefs, chauffeurs, chambermaids, royal treatment, gowns, jewelry, the highest of high-heels, and a tall glass of aristocratic hunk that would show me how it was to be a woman… even just for one night.

Clutch your Pearl Necklace Tight and Prepare for a Feminization Romance Ride!

Note: This collection contains feminization, transgender transformation, romance, and first time with a transgender woman tropes.

Read Feminization Fantasies

"I started giving up on life until she gave
up heaven so we could be together."

Read Angel Baby

Book Bundles

∞∞∞

Need more of my romantic bedtime stories? It's your lucky day! All of my bundles are unique, and none of the stories were cross-added so you can buy all of them without having to worry about whether or not a story already appeared on another bundle.

With these bundles, you're going to save more than 50%. Love love love!

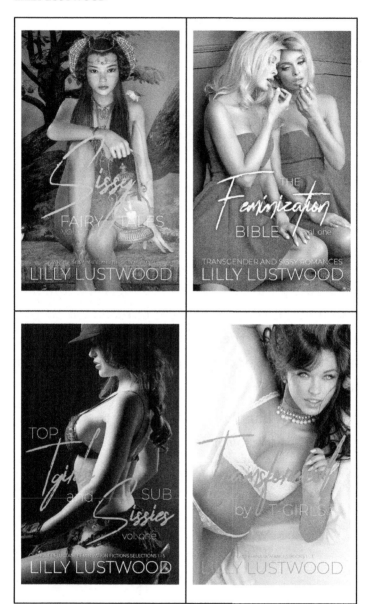

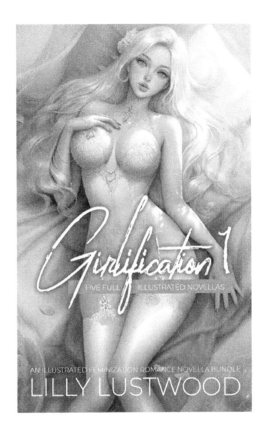

Custom Story

∞∞∞

Did you know that I also write custom/commission-based stories? Yes, I do, and I will write it to the tee based on your liking. Here's a sample of a commission story I've created for one of my lovely readers.

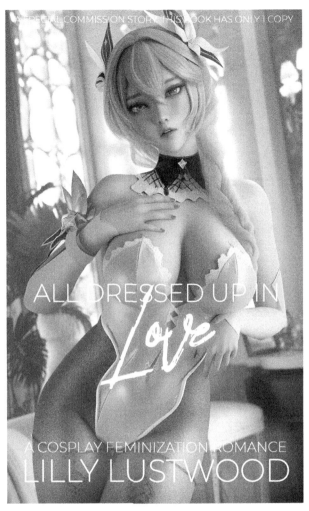

Added to that, if you're a Lilly Lustwood reader, you're quite aware of how colorful my prose is and I do three rounds of edits before I publish. Please understand that masterpieces cannot be rushed.

Don't take my word for it, here's what one of them had to say:

"I love the story!!!! Ty for writing almost 100 pages for Michelle and Evelynn—I'm sure they're happy you gave them such love and attention as well. <3 My only disappointment came when I finished reading, but I realized I can re-read as much as I want.

Your storytelling skills are so great—if there's any way I can leave a review please let me know! I truly enjoyed every moment of this commission." -Michelle

Get Your Own Story

Audiobooks

∞ ∞ ∞

I know that many of you prefer consuming a book while doing something else. Most especially when it's some of my books which are hard to read even with one hand haha!

That's why I've created audiobook versions of my top sellers. They're available on Audible and other major distributors!

Listen to Audiobooks

Sissy Store

SISSY TOYS & CLOTHES
FOR FEMININE BOYS

Many of my readers love dressing up. What inspired me to create the Sissy Store is the e-mails I've received from them wanting to emulate the characters in my story.

And the best way to do that? Dressing up of course! That's why I made the Sissy Store, it's a curation of my favorite finds online to provide you with an easier time in shopping for the best outfits available.

From wigs, breastplates, stockings, and down to shoes, toys, uniforms, lingerie, and more, you'll find everything you need!

Visit The Sissy Store

Other Titles

"The only Feminization Guide you'll ever need."

Read The Girly Guide 2

"Underneath her pencil skirt and silk blouse, distracting all the yearning men in the conference room with her apparition, she knew exactly who to give her attention to for her next career opportunity."

Read The Office Gurl

"There's that voice again… telling me to swipe the scarlet rouge on my lips, wear my mother's dress, and go to the nearest bar in my red stilettos".

Read Femininely Possessed

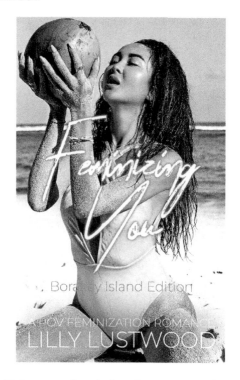

"It's your feminization story, I just
wrote it for you, xoxo Lilly."

Read Feminizing You

"I have two pieces of good news, first, you're not going to school anymore, and second, you're hired as a new maid!"

"My father wouldn't allow this!"

"Enough with the drama, slide on those Mary Janes!"

Read Sissyrella

Author's Message

Dear Romantic Reader,

Thank you very much for purchasing and reading *My Crazy Girl – Reluctant Feminization with College*

Sweetheart.

For a writer, I can't seem to find the best word to describe how grateful I am for your support.

If you enjoyed this book, KINDLY **(with puppy-dog eyes) give it a Rating and Review it on Kindle.**

Let's get it to the overall bestseller list <3

Should you feel the need to send me a message concerning this book, your love life, or just about anything, please feel free to follow the pages below and Subscribe to my Mailing List to get updates on Free Books, Promos, and New Releases.

You can also follow my author profile on Amazon simply by visiting the Amazon Page below, you will get e-mails from Amazon whenever I have a new book, xo.

Mailing List (stats.sender.net/forms/er756a/view)

Home Page (www.lillylustwood.wordpress.com)

Amazon Page (www.amazon.com/Lilly-Lustwood/e/B0B9X11BMR/)

Facebook | Twitter | TikTok (@LillyLustwood)

Goodreads (www.goodreads.com/lillylustwood)

Printed in Great Britain
by Amazon

40355115R00108